I0741741

The Daisy Chain

by

Diane Guntrip

Term 1 Entry 1

Dear H,

Well, the countdown is over! After all the waiting, I can now proudly boast to the world that I am a music student, specialising in Vocal Studies, at St Celia's Academy of Music. Isn't that cool?

Did you think I'd forgotten you? No way! It's just been so hectic here and I've been lost in a frenzy of activity. Have you ever felt like that? Everything is great, but I feel as though I've been uplifted to another universe and I'm spinning in a continuous whirlwind. I just need to stop the world for a short time to catch my breath.

Don't worry. It's not as bad as it sounds. I just wanted to touch base with you and let you know how I'm settling in. I'll give you all of the details when I've more time to write.

Wow!

Amanda

Term 1 Entry 2

Dear H,

Hurrah! At last, I've found some quiet time to sit down and write. Mum and Dad have now returned home to their hectic lives. My Mum is a successful owner of a chain of fashion boutiques and my Dad is a busy senior partner in a law firm. Remember, they travelled to the Academy with me? They stayed in a hotel close by for a few days to help me settle in as it's my first time away from home on my own. I was so grateful for this.

Awesome! It's a free Saturday afternoon, and I'm really relieved no organised activities have been planned. How I've been hanging out for some spare time! The pace, so far, has been hectic and I desperately need some time out. My head feels as though it's continually buzzing and ready to burst. It'll be much better when I'm in a routine. I have SO many things I want to share with you. I've been storing all of my new experiences in my head as well as scribbling them down in my notebook hoping I won't forget them.

I'm sure, sitting here and describing everything to you step by step, will help me put it all into perspective, calm me down and help me to organise my thoughts so that my mind won't appear to be in such a jumbled mess.

I'm upside down
Inside out
Strung out on a line so tight.
I'm living in a topsy-turvy world!
Need to get myself
Sorted out!

PHEW!! Time to take some slow breaths and remember the techniques Mrs Field, my singing teacher at home, taught me when I became a bit frazzled.

What must you be thinking of me? It's really not as bad as it sounds. I'm thrilled to be here, ecstatic in fact. It's just that St Celia's Academy is huge compared to my previous school, St Ursula's, and with the brand new school routine, the adrenalin has been working overtime. Apart from this, there has been the move from home and having to get used to living with lots of other girls in the boarding house. It's a completely new experience for me. I've always been used to my own space and spending time on my own so I have to get used to a completely different way of life. I will admit to you, and no one else, that it's not as easy as I imagined.

Now that I've got all of that out of the way, let me tell you all about it right from the start. I've a feeling that this is going to be a long diary entry!!

First of all, we had a five hour flight. We arrived at the hotel the night before the tour of the school and special early afternoon tea took place. This was arranged only for the new students and their parents. It was SO exciting that it passed in a complete blur. It was a shame that I couldn't absorb it all.

Mum, Dad and I were then shown up to my room in Grantham House. Ever since I heard I had won the scholarship I had been counting down the weeks. You can imagine that by now, my emotions had built up to a huge crescendo and I was walking on air. It wasn't until later, when Mum and Dad had returned to their hotel and I was in my room alone, that I suddenly crashed down to earth. I was hit with the realisation that I was on my own to cope with this new situation. Well, not completely on my own as I had the support of my parents, Gran and Emma but they weren't going to be with me personally on this very exciting journey. I've got to keep reminding myself to keep positive and follow the dream.

Now, Amanda, keep on track!

I'd been allocated my room on the second floor of Grantham House. It contains a single bed, desk and chair, chest of drawers and bookcase, fitted wardrobe AND my own ensuite! Can you believe it? I'm incredibly lucky.

I was busy unpacking my possessions from home, arranging

framed photos of Mum, Dad, Gran and Emma on the empty shelves and pinning my favourite posters on the large cork board when I suddenly became aware of lots of frantic activity further along the corridor. I could hear doors banging, girls screaming in delight, presumably on meeting up with best friends again after the long summer break. I felt quite sad and a bit lost and I had the first tiny pangs of home-sickness. All I wished for, at that moment, was a friend of my own to greet me.

I bravely continued with my unpacking, finished it and then realised I didn't know what I was supposed to do or what was expected of me. Had I missed out on some vital piece of information? Had I been told what was going to happen after I'd unpacked? I racked my brain. I just couldn't remember. My mind appeared completely empty.

I sat down quickly on the bed as I realised, just thinking about it all, had made me feel sick in the stomach and my legs had turned to jelly. I'd heard of people using that expression before but never really knew what it meant. Now I know! I'd never been in this situation before and I felt completely out of my depth. For an instant, all my old fears returned. You remember what I was like when I attended St Ursula's? All sorts of doubts suddenly emerged. I felt swamped with anxiety. I had to remind myself that this was what I had been waiting for all this time. Just at that moment, I wasn't sure I was doing the right thing.

What really scared me was whether I would make friends. It sounds awful to admit that I never had any friends in my previous life at the awful St Ursula's. No one there seemed to be like me or understand me. In fact, I didn't have a real friend until I met Emma, a student from a nearby school, who shared my love of singing. I wish she was here with me now. She's so easy to talk to. I've arranged to Skype her later on today.

Well, silly me, I need not have worried. The next moment, one of the Housemothers gently knocked on my door, popped her head around and said, "Hello Amanda. Welcome to St C's, I'm Gillie, one of your Housemothers. All the girls on this floor are coming along to the lounge room at the end of the corridor for a get-together. Please come. Everyone is dying to meet you. See you in five minutes."

I felt Gillie's friendliness wrap around me like a warm comforting blanket. She had such a lovely open smile and such deep brown eyes. Her fair hair was tied up in a pony tail and she was wearing jeans, sweatshirt and sneakers. Nothing formal about her and certainly not what I expected. None of the teaching staff at St Ursula's would have been seen dead in anything less than formal jackets and skirts.

I immediately felt my spirits begin to rise and the weight on my shoulders became a little lighter. I felt as though the new more confident Amanda I had become during the last few months was

SLOWLY beginning to surface. So, I plucked up my courage, took some deep slow breaths, put a smile on my face and I went. It was all very informal. There must have been about fifteen girls of differing ages, from thirteen up to nearly eighteen. They were all perched on any available space they could find. Some of the older girls appeared very poised and confident. Gillie suggested that I squeeze in next to another new girl who I had briefly noticed earlier in the day. Looking around, you could easily pick out the new girls by their frightened expressions. I probably appeared the same when I entered the room. I think the expression would be that we all looked like frightened rabbits!

Gillie began to speak, "Welcome everyone, especially the new students. It's great to see everyone here, safe and sound after the long summer break. For those of you who don't know, I'm Gillie one of your Housemothers. I also teach Song Writing. I'd like to welcome you to come to see me at any time if you need to chat about anything. Now, everyone, it's time for introductions."

The older girls started the ball rolling and I sat there trying to remember names, but it was hopeless. There were just too many new things going on that I couldn't take it all in. I wondered if I was the only one experiencing this or whether the other new girls were experiencing similar feelings. However, I found out, through the introductions, that some of the girls had flown in from overseas to attend the Academy. I thought it would be fun to get to know them, especially as we all share a love of music.

At that moment, I imagined a wonderful picture of us all getting on so well, encouraging and supporting each other. This idea was shattered by the late arrival of another girl who appeared to be about sixteen. She burst into the room announcing loudly in a haughty manner, "For those new students who don't know, my name is Jessica, NOT Jess. I'm an accomplished pianist. I'll be studying piano at the Conservatorium in London the year after next!"

This was greeted by the older girls with what I would describe as looks of distain. One of them replied, "I didn't know you'd been accepted at the Conservatorium."

Jessica replied snappily, "Well, of course, I'll be accepted!"

I overheard someone mutter, "Why does she always appear to be so irritating?"

I looked towards the girl sitting next to me and I could instantly tell from the look in her eyes, that she was also feeling wary of the newcomer. There was something about the latest arrival. She seemed to be over exuberant and full of her own importance. I had an awful feeling that I wasn't going to get on with her and hoped our paths wouldn't cross.

Anyway, returning to the get-together, Gillie explained, "As is usual on the first night of term, we have the disco to which everyone is invited. For newcomers, I'm sure some of the older girls will fill you in on time, place etc."

I thought to myself, "Oh no!"

You may think I'm odd. I know I'm thirteen but I'm just not used to having boys around as I attended an all girls' college and not having any brothers or close male relatives. I didn't feel very confident about attending the disco, especially on the first evening when I didn't know anyone. Gillie mentioned that as an alternative for anyone who decided that they didn't want to attend the disco, was that they could meet her in the lounge at the end of the corridor for a sing-a-long. I thought that sounded more my scene.

After the introductions, I found out that the girl sitting next to me was called Immie, short for Imogen. I had noticed her at the afternoon tea with her parents. She looked about my age but appeared very sophisticated. Everyone began to enthusiastically dive into the sandwiches, tiny iced cupcakes and other delicious treats except for Immie and myself who had already feasted earlier in the afternoon. However, I did accept a sandwich so as not to appear rude. It seemed as though everyone's nervous energy began to settle as we all became engrossed in non-stop noisy chatter.

I found out Immie's room was next to mine and she's here to

study piano. She told me that her father worked for one of the major airlines and that the family was based for the time being in Singapore. "You are brave coming all this way," I said.

"I'm used to it as I've always attended boarding school," she said. "My flight was only a bit longer than yours. Now that there's Skype, it helps a lot."

Later, as we sauntered back along the corridor to our rooms, Immie said, "I'll see you at dinner. I'll knock on your door when it's time and we can go down together."

"Oh, that would be great! See you later," I replied thankfully.

I hope I didn't sound too enthusiastic, but I was SO relieved. Immie appeared so calm and confident. I didn't want to admit to her that I had been dreading entering a large dining room all by myself. I also wondered if I would have any appetite left after two afternoon teas in one day. I thought I'll have to take care in the future if afternoon tea was a regular thing. No way am I going to return to being fat and frumpy ever again, but that's another story.

I must take a break now and Skype Emma. I promised her I would fill her in on the latest developments.
Hopefully, I'll have time to continue this later this evening.
Amanda

Term 1 Entry 3

Dear H,

Sorry I had to break off like that. I had a really good chat
with Emma. I don't know what I would do without you and
Emma. I'm just one of those people who need to talk-out my
problems on a one-to-one basis. If you remember, Emma is
the first friend I ever made and is my inspiration for singing.
I will always be so grateful to her. Without her, I wouldn't be
here. If I had not heard her sing, I would not have made
the decision to ask Gran to organise and pay for my singing
lessons with Mrs Field.

Emma still has lessons with Mrs Field. She has a marvellous
earthy voice very suited to singing jazz classics. She was
involved in a horrific horse riding accident and is now a
paraplegic. She's almost sixteen and is still a student at
Cranfield High.

Now returning to the story as promised, Immie arrived and
we went down for dinner. It was served cafeteria style in
the Dining Room on the ground floor. We share this with the
boys from Sherwood House. As I wandered along, clutching
my tray, I was relieved to find there was a huge choice of
food. Great! Tuna and salad was just what I was looking for!
If I sound a bit stuffy you'll understand that I used to be
terribly overweight. It doesn't take much for me to vividly

remember how it affected my self-esteem. I never, ever want to hear anyone call me 'Piggy' again! This was the name that I was called at St Ursula's. It hurt me more than I can ever express. This is the reason I'm not willing to allow myself to return to being overweight and unhealthy ever again. I won't even mention how depressed I felt. All of that is finished with!

Tables seat eight, but Immie and I managed to jag one in a corner where no one else was sitting and it was great getting to know her. She's very easy to talk to, very similar to Emma, and we were very soon absorbed in girl talk! Thankfully, whilst we were chatting, Immie mentioned that she wasn't keen on attending the disco either, so I didn't feel such a spoil sport.

I was so thrilled that I had met a new friend! What a relief! Mum will be really pleased when I tell her.

After dinner, Immie and I both wandered along to the lounge at the end of our floor where Gillie was playing her guitar and singing. We were joined by a few more girls, from other floors, which was great. We didn't want to stand out as being the only ones not to attend the disco. Gillie has a marvellous voice, so rich and velvety. I suddenly remembered where I had heard her name before and realised that she is a famous lyricist. She played some songs that we all knew and I really enjoyed joining in. Fingers crossed that she'll be my Song Writing tutor.

Well, that brings you up to date with my first day at St C's. What an action packed day it has been! I left Gillie's singsong early and fell fast asleep dreaming of another exciting day to follow.

Walking tall!

Love from Amanda

Term 1 Entry 4

Dear H,

Remember the awful uniform I used to have to wear at St Ursula's? It used to make me feel as though I was a large bulging parcel tied up tightly with string around my middle! I must have looked hideous! Words fail to express how much I hated that uniform. I am so relieved I no longer have to wear that dingy green top which bleached every ounce of colour from my face and that awful brown pleated skirt that made me look huge around my middle. NEVER AGAIN will I wear brown!

Well, listen to this! This one is completely different. I think I mentioned to you before that it was blue. We all have a polo shirt in two-toned blue. With this, we are allowed to wear, wait for it... SMART BLUE JEANS! I couldn't believe it when I read about it in the Academy hand book. Thankfully, now that I've lost some weight, I can wear these without feeling uncomfortable. There's also a blue skirt as an option for winter, which is thankfully not pleated but more of an A line. For summer, there is also a smart pair of tailored shorts for girls, but I haven't seen anyone wearing shorts even though it's hot at the moment. When it's cold, there is a smart blue jacket, the same for boys and girls. When it's really cold and wet, there's a heavier quilted, waterproof version of the jacket. No straw boaters, lace up shoes and ankle socks!

Wicked!

Settling in and enjoying life,

Love Amanda

Term 1 Entry 5

Dear H,

Last night, the college held a special welcome barbeque for all of the new students. We were all expected to attend, so I couldn't avoid going. I'm still getting those 'tap dancing' butterflies in my tummy every time I'm faced with something new, but this time, I felt more confident knowing that I'd have Immie by my side. In fact, did those butterflies signal a flutter of excitement? I think you could say it did. Is this really Amanda talking?

We only have to wear school uniform during school hours. The news of the barbeque created lots of excitement coupled with chatter and laughter, amongst the new girls on the corridor. Conversations as to what they were going to wear, how to do their hair, and what colour nail varnish to use, took place. This was totally alien to me. I suppose someone with sisters would have been used to this, but in my former life at St. Ursula's, it was something I'd never experienced before. It's something else for me to get used to.

Immie would make a fabulous model. She is tall for her age and very slim and willowy with long auburn hair and brown eyes. She doesn't look as if she's ever suffered from having pimples on her face. She has a beautiful clear complexion. Can you remember when I began writing to you, how I moaned about my spots? Thankfully, that's all in the past. I wouldn't class myself as model material but I am more accepting of myself. I've begun to realise that it's the person inside and NOT what they look like that is important.

Well, back to the topic. I do get side-tracked don't I? Immie kept popping in and out of my room, wearing a different outfit each time.

She asked, "What do you think to this?"

"I think that's awesome," I replied, "Really cool!"

By the time she'd repeated this six times, I began to think I'd never manage to get myself changed and ready. Thankfully, and with only a short time left, Immie decided she'd wear a new pair of cream linen pants and a casual top in a coppery colour which featured a bold design. She added a copper bracelet with lots of charms and glittery beads and matching earrings. These were THE FIRST clothes she had put on that evening before all the changing took place! I thought to myself, "I think being a friend of Immie's is going to be FUN!"

I quickly decided to wear a pair of white jeans combined with a swirly top in my favourite sea green. Of course, I wore my Daisy Chain pendant which Immie admired. We each added a tiny bit of make-up as it was a special occasion and told ourselves we looked cool. To celebrate we took our first selfies together. I have since sent a copy to Mum. She was thrilled to receive it. I felt relieved and thrilled myself.

The barbeque was being held in the courtyard of Sherwood House, the boys' residence. The first thing that hit us as we walked towards the courtyard was a strong aroma of onions, steak and sizzling sausages. On arrival, we found that a few of the older students were in charge of arranging the barbeque, along with a couple of the Housemasters and Housemothers who were on duty that evening. I was really surprised to find fairy lights had been strung around some of the exposed beams in the courtyard which really helped to create a party atmosphere, as did the water feature, containing coloured lights at its base.

Mum would have been most impressed. You know how she likes a party! Although, come to think of it, she would have had to have a theme if she'd been organising this evening. I dread to think what it might have been!

I noticed a temporary stage had been set up in one corner of the courtyard complete with sound equipment. Everyone was really excited and there was a definite buzz in the air.

After we'd all finished eating and talking non-stop, four of the senior guys walked up onto the stage and collected their instruments and, after much tuning of guitars and testing of the microphones, they began to perform. They were terrific. There was a keyboard player, a drummer and two guitarists, who each took it in turns to sing. During the introduction, a member of the band told us that they enjoyed getting together to play modern music as a way to relax from their classical music studies. They call themselves RELIEF!

It did not take long before everyone began to join in singing and dancing. Can you believe it? Immie dragged me from the corner insisting I join in with the dancing! It felt strange at first. I felt very self conscious until I realised that no one was really taking any notice of me as they were all too busy enjoying themselves.

I must make some quick Skype calls before I go to bed. Is there such a thing as a quick Skype call? Perhaps I'd better leave it until tomorrow, otherwise I'll be up all night!

Goodnight, from a happy and relaxed 'sleepyhead'!

Amanda

Term 1 Entry 6

Dear H,

I've been so busy chatting about what I've been doing that I'd completely forgotten I hadn't described the Academy to you. As you already know, St C's is a specialist music college. The full name is, St Celia's Academy of Music for Talented and Gifted Students. That's a real mouthful isn't it? That's why it shortened to St C's. I didn't realise until I'd won the competition that Cecelia is the Patron Saint of Music. Celia is a shortened form of the name, except we've shortened it even further!!

According to the Academy brochure sent before I arrived, it says the school buildings are based around a beautiful historic home built in the early 1800s called Franklin House. It is set in extensive parkland and was originally owned by a wealthy, business family named Humphrey-Bond whose portraits still hang in the hall.

Apart from their successful businesses, the family were Patrons of the Arts and strangely enough, the wife of the first owner of the house was also called Celia. It appears the house was handed down through the generations, and as the last male heir had no children, he left all of his money to be used for the upkeep and continued running of the Academy.

This magnificent old house is really something. Emma would fall in love with it. I must describe it to her and take lots of photos. I suppose, as I get used to the building, that I won't be quite so blown away by its splendour. I can't believe how lucky I am to attend such a school.

The building has been updated and includes central heating, air-conditioning, electric lighting and modern bathroom facilities, but the original carved wood and stone fireplaces still remain.

I'm quite swept away with all of this as you can tell. I must be boring you with all of these details and my ramblings. I just want to give you an idea of what my new life is like and the surroundings in which I'm now living. The original house is now set up as a traditional school, with the rooms being used as classrooms, library, art room, science labs and administration offices. The original ballroom is where we have weekly assemblies. It's really awesome.

Something that I have had to get used to is the early start! We begin lessons at 8am, finishing at 2pm. Of course, we have a short break mid morning and a longer break later for lunch. You might think, well that's great, but then the real reason we are here is to study MUSIC. We have our specialised music lessons for the remainder of the afternoon, except for Wednesday, when it's Sport.

"Oh no! Poor Amanda!" I can hear you say, but don't worry. It's something else to tell you later. Some evenings there are also rehearsals for the choir etc. So you could say it's full on.

Feeling inspired and so fortunate,

Love Amanda

PS Reminder: take some photos of the House for Emma and Gran.

Term 1 Entry 7

Dear H,

I think I remember mentioning Wednesday afternoons are dedicated to Sport. The first week this happened, I approached it with dread. You know about my ideas on Sport and the terrible time I had at my previous school. I had heard and read about the Sport Options but thought they sounded too good to be true. BUT NO! It is true and it's marvellous! What a relief! We are allowed to choose from a list of Options, but it's first come, first served and you can't repeat your Option more than once in a year. Now, listen to this!

SPORTS OPTIONS

<u>Yoga and Meditation</u> - would possibly help me to relax, certainly give it a go.

<u>Nordic Bush Walking</u> - that's walking with poles, have you seen them? Think I may enjoy it as long as the pace isn't too fast and there aren't too many hills! I think this is a winter one owing to the heat in the early afternoon.

<u>Ten pin bowling</u> - I've never tried this, may be a possibility, sounds fun!

<u>Swimming</u> - we're taken to the local pool. I'm not keen on water; don't like to put my head under!

Cycling - bikes can be hired! Think I'll put this as my first Option! Second thoughts, it may be too hot in the middle of the day.

Roller-blading - think I'll give it a miss!

Zumba - would like to give this a try, but only if Immie goes with me!

Dance - just for fun! Hip-hop, jazz, salsa, just to name a few. This sounds good, especially if I audition for musicals later on.

Gym - the bus takes a group to a local gym. Doesn't inspire me! Too many memories of the gym at St Ursula's!!

As we aren't a specialised Sports College and our teachers are biased towards academia and music, most of the Options are taken by visiting coaches. For anyone who wishes to play an organised sport, such as Netball, Soccer etc, the school arranges for those students to join a team organised by another school or community group.

I've not decided yet what to do. I'll let you know later.

From a 'trim and terrific'
Amanda
PS Well I will be when I've accomplished some of the above!!

Term 1 Entry 8

Dear H,

My vocal lessons, which are the reason I'm here, are now in full swing. My vocal tutor is Mrs Emily Blake. You may have heard of her. She's similar to Mrs Field in that she has appeared on the world stage taking the lead roles in numerous musicals and as a solo performer. She has semi-retired for the time being as she has a young family and wants to spend lots of time with them. However, she still appears on TV and performs occasionally. I really like her now that I'm getting to know her.

My first lesson wasn't the best though. You know me, I'm filled with doubts and never think I'm good enough. I was really nervous and it showed in my voice, almost as bad as when I had my first lesson with Mrs Field. Mrs Blake immediately realised I was nervous and instead of continuing the singing, sat down and had a chat with me. She told me to not have doubts about my ability. She said, "Amanda, if you didn't have talent, you wouldn't have been offered a scholarship. Don't ever forget that."

I thanked her for being so understanding and vowed I would do better next time. I didn't feel too pleased with myself. I felt as though I had let myself down. I returned to my room feeling flat, disappointed and angry with myself. I immediately rang Gran for a chat. Gran is my Fairy Godmother. She doesn't wave a wand, but she certainly knows how to make you feel better.

"Amanda, we've been through this before. It's just that you've had so many new experiences to cope with. You'll do better next time. You have a very special gift. There is no reason to feel nervous."

Thankfully, the rest of my singing lessons have been great fun and I'm enjoying them immensely. As my voice is still developing, I'm learning different styles of singing, except for opera, which doesn't appeal to me. Next year I will have to make a decision as to what I want to specialise in.

I've also started my Song Writing option and yes, Gillie, or should I say, Ms Longhirst is my tutor. For this option, I'm in a small group of six students of mixed ages. We are concentrating on writing song lyrics. For our first project, Ms Longhirst recommended we write about something that we feel is important to us. In that way, we already have firsthand experience and so can express our deepest feelings. I immediately knew what my topic was going to be. Can you guess? The idea and a few words are already buzzing around in my head. I'll share it with you later when I've worked on it. Feeling more confident.
Amanda

PS I've been so busy I forgot to tell you that I decided to stick with something safe for my Sports Option. I know it's not very exciting but I chose Cycling. I feel confident with cycling, I enjoy it and I know it keeps me keep fit and trim.

Term 1 Entry 9

Dear H,

You remember the problems that I had with texts and vicious emails at St Ursula's and how I used to leave my phone in the cupboard at home switched off? Well, thankfully, at St C's, mobile phone use is banned during lesson times. Any student found to be using a phone is in big trouble! Parents are instructed to phone the Academy directly if there is an emergency. During the day, phones have to be locked away. iPads are required for certain lessons but there are strict regulations regarding their use. However, this isn't quite so easy to monitor.

As you can imagine, as soon as the girls return to Grantham House after lessons have finished, they all race to their phones and for about 15 minutes, there is absolute silence whilst they check all of their social networks and reply to their messages. Afterwards, they nearly all appear with their headphones, mostly deep pink in colour, clamped to their ears. Sometimes, it's difficult to start up a conversation. We end up using a kind of sign language.

Can you remember the pink phone Mum bought me for my last birthday? I still keep it locked away unless I'm checking for news from Mum, Gran and Emma. I still haven't been able to rid myself of the fear of the cruel texts that Cassandra sent me. I'm probably being silly but I have refused to share my mobile number or personal email address with anyone here yet. Not even Immie has them. I know everyone thinks I'm a bit strange doing this. I've received a few comments about me being odd and I do feel unsociable carrying this out. So far, I've kept the reason to myself. If anyone persists with questions, I reply, "My friends are people I actually know and want to be friends with."

Thankfully, that has satisfied everyone so far.

I'd much rather have a handful of proper friends I can rely on than 200 who I really don't know at all. As for my iPad, if I see a name or address which I don't recognise, I delete it.

Keeping safe and being extra cautious,

Amanda

Term 1 Entry 10

Dear H,

I've received an email from Emma. She tells me that she has heard via the grapevine, (through a friend of a friend ... you know what I mean) that the cold, calculating Cassandra, backed by her 'colleagues in crime', is still up to her tricks at St Ursula's. It made me feel icy cold just to hear Cassandra's name mentioned. I began to feel sick in the stomach, cold and sweaty at the same time. It brings back so many awful memories. She is the greatest bully I know and was the cause of countless incidents that caused me heartbreak and made my life a living nightmare. I don't want to have anything more to do with her ever again.

It would appear that Cassandra has now set her sights on another student at St Ursula's. She's new, rather small for her age and hasn't, as yet, made any friends. The girl has frequently been seen crying and distressed on her way home from school. I can never work out how Cassandra gets away with it. Emma tells me she will keep me updated.

Emma, along with Gran, was my great support throughout the latter part of Cassandra's intimidation of me. She helped me to cope with the constant bullying and gave me advice on how to deal with it. Emma also stressed that it was Cassandra who had the problem and not me. She introduced me to the Daisy Chain, a school support group whose members are always there for each other.

Before I left to come here, Emma presented me with a silver daisy pendant on a chain. It is the symbol for anti-bullying and my most treasured possession. I wear it under my polo top at all times. It gives me strength and that if I ever hear of anyone being bullied, I will befriend them and give them support. Luckily, we are allowed to wear small stud earrings and small pendants on chains.

The Daisy Chain also helped in narrowing the huge gap that had existed between my parents and me. They had absolutely no idea that I had been the subject of such intense daily bullying until Emma presented me with the pendant. Although it was a complete shock to my Mum, finding out about the bullying helped to bring us closer together. It taught us both of the value of quality conversation and of the importance of putting time aside daily to discuss and share our problems.

Remembering the times I sat alone,
Cooped up in my room,
Talking to myself
With feelings of despair and gloom.

Remembering the thoughts inside my head,
Bouncing to and fro,
Fogging up my brain.
Endless chatter, nowhere to go.

Reminding myself to appreciate
What I know is true.
Sharing is power,
Strength gained from when I talk with you.

Feeling strong!
Amanda

Term 1 Entry 11

Dear H,

I can't believe it. I've been here all this time and not told you about the MOST important building in the Academy, the MUSIC BLOCK usually called the BLOCK! When I first entered the Music Block, with Mum and Dad on the tour around the college. Awesome! I had not expected it to be so out of this world. So 'gobsmacked' with it, I must have stood there with my mouth wide open like a goldfish until Mum nudged me and whispered, "Amanda, close your mouth darling." To think that I had been chosen and given the chance to study at such a brilliant venue blew me away. I felt quite emotional and had to delve into my bag for a tissue.

Our entire music lessons take place in this state-of-the-art architecturally designed building adjacent to Franklin Hall. There we have small sound-proof rooms, some containing pianos, where we can practise our instruments and sing to raise the roofs. We can make as much noise as required without interfering or irritating other students who are practising or rehearsing.

There are larger rooms of varying sizes set up for group work and rehearsals such as when the string quartet gets together. The choir, of which I'm a member, also performs in such a room. Then there is the large concert hall, acoustically balanced and supporting a grand piano on its raised stage. This is where we hold our end of semester concerts twice a year. These are grand affairs, I've been told, where the girls dress formally in blue shimmery dresses (thankfully, not pink... my least favourite colour) and the boys in dark suits and matching blue satin bow ties. Can you imagine the scene?

Our parents and the general public are invited to these. I've been told the tickets sell out fast so must remind Mum, Dad and Gran to order their tickets early.

Apart from Vocal Studies, there are tutors for Dance and Instrumental etc. There's one last room in the Block I must mention, and that is the RECORDING STUDIO!! Can you imagine! I'm told it has as much recording equipment as any major studio and of the same high quality. No wonder there is a security system in place and a team of security guards who tour the grounds both during the day and at night! It would make my day if I could go in there and record one of the songs I've written.

My mind was suddenly jolted back and I remembered a verse from one of the songs I wrote before I came here, 'Fabulous Superstar!' Can you remember it?

> I am the sun, the star
> Ready to shine.
> I must stretch out

Aim high as the sky.
Better to fail
Than never to try.

At that moment I decided I was going to 'aim high as the sky'.

We've all got to dream!

Love from Amanda

Term 1 Entry 12

Dear H,

The Academy is situated on the outskirts of a village. It only takes 5 minutes for us to walk to the village where there are a few local shops and a Post Office - nothing really special. You need to travel to the closest town, a twenty minute bus ride away for more choice, and to the city, an hour away, if serious shopping is on your mind!

It's usual to see the houses in the area having 'equestrian facilities', which is a posh way of saying they have enough land for stables and ponies on their properties! It gives you an idea of the sort of area the Academy is located.

The Academy owns a mini bus which, on a Saturday, offers us a free return trip into the small nearby town. We have to go with a friend and not to forget to sign the register on the ground floor of our residence before leaving and when we return.

Yesterday, Saturday, Immie and I went on our first organised trip into the actual city. A group of us, plus a couple of the teaching staff went to watch the stage musical, 'Grease' at the theatre. As it was only a small group, we travelled together on the local service bus which slowly snaked its way along the leafy country lanes and stopped to pick up or drop passengers in each village on its way. With all of the stops and starts, it took us about an hour and a half but it was great fun, lots of chatter and laughter all the way there and back! A few of the boys went too. I'm beginning to get used to having them around. Some of them are great teases and really funny. Never having had a brother, I'm not used to this. I find I'm quite enjoying it. I can't believe I'm saying this!!

I think one of the guys, Patrick, is keen on Immie. He has started to talk and joke with her and somehow, he managed to position himself to sit next to her in the theatre. She kept turning to me, as I was sitting on her right side, and completely ignored the poor guy on her left. He tried a few times to start up a conversation, but she played 'hard to get'. I felt quite sorry for him. However, Immie says she has come to the Academy to study piano and her intention is to go on to study at the Conservatorium in either London or New York. She's very serious about it and states that nothing is going to get in the way of her dream, but at the same time, I think she was secretly enjoying the attention. Watch this space!

Talking about boyfriends, one of the girls on our corridor, Tilly, short for Matilda, has a boyfriend who she is always talking about. She appears to be constantly on edge waiting for replies to the texts she has sent him. The cork board, in her room, is covered with photos of them together. She has almost deserted her best friend Amy and spends all of her free time with him. His name is Jacques, and according to Tilly, he's just perfect. She tells everyone she met him in the only cafe in the village and it's hot gossip that she secretly meets up with him quite often. He has a car and Tilly somehow manages to avoid the security guys and sneak out of the school grounds to meet him in the evenings. So far, the Academy appears not to know about her evening dates. I don't know how long she'll be able to continue without being found out.

Anyway, I got a bit carried away there! After the theatre, we had some free time. Immie announced loudly, "Amanda and I are going to look at clothes in that amazing boutique up the road."

Her new found friend, Patrick, took the hint and walked off in the opposite direction. Actually, Immie and I escaped to a store where we both found some amazing bracelets to add to our already large collections of funky jewellery and then we all returned to school. I really enjoyed it. I'm gradually getting to know more people but think I'll always prefer spending time with one or two close friends than be part of a large group. I feel more comfortable being with one or two people, it's just the way I am.

Feeling contented,

Amanda

Term 1 Entry 13

Dear H,

Ever since I attended my first Song Writing session, my thoughts have been swirling around in my head. I've begun to scribble numerous phases in my notebook as the ideas have come to me. So far, I think I've got an idea for the first verse.

> Little daisy
> Standing alone
> In a field with a greenish hue,
> Battered by the wind and rain.
>
> Is that you?
>
> Is that you?

Well, it's getting there! The rest is hovering around in my head. I have an idea of what I want to say. I've just got to wait until it appears. I don't normally sit down with the intention of writing my song lyrics. Instead I wait for the ideas to form in my head. Then it's scribble, scribble before I forget. They usually arrive at inconvenient times like whilst I'm having a shower or riding my bike.

Talking of bullying, everyone 'appears' to be getting on with

each other fairly well at the moment. You would think that
as we all love music in one form or another we'd all be there
to support each other. BUT NO! I think I see a few worrying
cracks appearing. Have you noticed that when you are in a new
situation, everyone appears to be on their best behaviour?
They either seem to be trying to assess the sort of person
you are or are trying madly to impress you. It's after that
stage that problems, if they are going to occur, could begin.

Some of the older students really think they are superior.
They walk around, in catwalk style, with their heads held high
swishing their hair from side to side. They certainly know how
to show their disapproval if they hear of anyone else being
praised, by the awful things they say, usually loud enough for
you to hear. I've quickly learnt not to 'step on their toes',
talk about inflated egos!

Immie has been studying piano since she was 4 years
old. She has a natural gift but her high standard of
performance is also due to all the hours she has put into
practising. She told me that Jessica, who we met on the
first evening, and who is presently applying for a place to
study classical piano at the Conservatorium in London, (or
somewhere equally famous and prestigious) told Immie that
she'd heard her playing. In her opinion, Immie would never
be good enough to be a concert pianist. She continued by
saying that she thought Immie was wasting her time being

at the Academy and was taking up the place of someone who had REAL talent, (I DON'T THINK SO!). She added that it wasn't just her, but a lot of other people were of the same opinion. Who these 'other people' are, I'm not sure, but no one else has come forward to support Jessica. It was interesting that Jessica made these comments when no one was around to hear her apart from Immie.

Fortunately, Immie is very sensible and has come across comments such as this before. She just put on her normal ravishing smile, didn't respond and walked away with her head held high. I congratulated her on her response. Another student may have taken the comment the wrong way and been devastated.

It wasn't until after Immie had shared the details with me of her distressing encounter with Jessica that I plucked up my courage and confided in Immie. I told her the whole sorry story of my miserable history at St Ursula's. Her response was one of surprise, "But you always appear so confident."

Immie's words made me feel great, a real confidence booster. I didn't tell her that I sometimes put on an act of appearing confident.

I showed Immie my silver daisy pendant and talked about its symbolic meaning. She suggested that if we ever heard or saw evidence of anyone being bullied at St C's, we would start a Daisy Chain group and be there to give our support. I must tell Emma about this. I am so fortunate to have Immie as my college friend.

Thankful for friendship,

Amanda

Term 1 Entry 14

Dear H,

School work is progressing well. All of the students know that St C's is a very special place. We have to work hard in order to achieve good grades. We are reminded that there are plenty of other students who would willingly take our place. That's not to say we don't have fun. It's not always serious here and we are encouraged to play hard as well as work hard.

However, we have to take our music VERY seriously. I can't believe that it's nearly the end of Term One. Preparations are in place for the first concert of the year. Remember, I mentioned that these concerts are held twice a year. The first will be held during the last week of Term Two. I'm busy practising two songs to sing as solos and the choir is rehearsing like mad. Our music is being played on the piano whilst we rehearse, but at the concert, we'll be accompanied by the full orchestra. It's all very exciting but terrifying at the same time.

Mum and Dad, as well as Gran, have ordered their tickets and will be attending.

Can't wait!

Amanda

PS Really excited! The Academy has announced that it is employing a company to produce a live webinar of the concert. This will be great for parents of students from overseas, who aren't able to attend the concert. They will now be able to watch online. This means that Emma will be able to watch. It's great that she won't feel left out.

Term 1 Entry 15

Dear H,

Song Writing! For some reason, I've been having problems. I know what I want to say but the words have been spinning around in space. I've lots of phrases written in a small turquoise leather bound notebook. Gran gave it to me. I carry it everywhere so I can jot down ideas when I think of them. Anyway, I've managed to put some thoughts together. This is what I've come up with so far. I'm a bit concerned about the reaction of the group when I present this to them.

The Daisy Chain

Little daisy
Standing alone
In a field with a greenish hue,
Battered by the wind and rain.
Is that you?
Is that you?

Little daisy
Standing forlorn
Ready waiting to be reborn,
Left to nature's beck and call.
Trampled, torn,
Trampled torn.

Little daisy
How many seeds
Scattered throughout on hill and plain
Nurtured by the gentle rain?
Daisy Chain,
Daisy Chain.

Chorus
Step by step, side by side
Come join the Daisy Chain.
Join us and we'll be your guide
Help you hold your head up high.
Together, we'll step out, speak out,
Fight the foe
And put the bullies to shame.
Come, don't be afraid
Join the Daisy Chain!

The Song Writing group meets tomorrow, so not long to wait.

Fingers crossed.

Amanda

Term 1 Entry 16

Dear H,

At last, it was my turn to present my song. I had sat
and listened to the lyrics of all the songs written by the
other students in the group. They all sounded pretty special
to me. I was 'lucky last' being the youngest student in
the group. I was really impressed especially by the songs
written by the older students and Gillie's comments were
so positive and encouraging. I was really nervous sharing
my song with the rest of the group. The feeling that the
song wasn't good enough was circulating in my head and
I felt a bit sick. I'm still troubled by my nerves on certain
occasions. I could feel my heart beating really fast and my
hands were clammy.

I had a tune in mind, so thought it may sound better if I
sang the words. When I'd finished, there was deathly silence. I
sat there looking at the expressions on everyone's faces and
asking myself, "What have I done?"

Simon, one of the older guys in the group, broke the silence
with, "Amanda that was tremendous. What inspired you to
write such an emotional song? You sounded as though you
meant every word you sang."

Gillie followed this up with, "Amanda, that was a great first attempt. Would you like to share with us your reasons for writing this song?"

My first reaction was to be thrilled by their response to the song and immediately, a sense of relief flooded through my body. This was quickly followed by a feeling of being trapped. I did not intend to share with the group the reasons why I had written the song. However, six pairs of eyes settled upon me waiting expectantly. I sat there, glued to the seat, wishing that I was a million miles away. I felt my face begin to burn with embarrassment. No way was I going to avoid their questioning. Hesitantly, the story of my bullying came out. I didn't find it easy sharing my story with strangers. I'm naturally a very private person and prefer to choose who I confide in. I didn't really know them and was concerned about their reactions. Would they think I was weak because I'd been bullied? Would they then start the bullying off again? I could tell by the expressions on their faces that they were concerned. Did they feel sorry for me? I hope not. I began hesitantly, but once I started, found that I couldn't stop and the whole story came out.

Our Song Writing session turned out to be more of a 'heart to heart'. Simon, who was a guitarist in the band RELIEF and normally so confident, wasn't able to look anyone in the face. He was so embarrassed that he kept his eyes firmly fixed on a spot on the floor whilst continually shuffling his feet on the carpet and wringing his hands together. I really felt uncomfortable as I realised how he was feeling. Hesitantly, he told us his story of how he'd also been bullied when he was seven years of age whilst a boarder at a Prep school. He confided that he'd never spoken to anyone else about it before but that it had been one of the worst periods in his life. He said, the words of my song had really touched him. They had brought back the terrible feelings he'd experienced all those years ago which he'd hidden away in the back of his mind. I admired him for being so brave.

Gillie told us that everything that had been shared that afternoon would be private and confidential and that we were not to discuss it with other students. I said a silent thank you and breathed a sigh of relief.

I did, however, mention the Daisy Chain group and showed them my silver daisy pendant. I shared the symbolism behind the pendant and left the idea of the Daisy Chain as a suggestion. Almost like an idea that others may want to take further if required.

By this time, our lesson had gone on twice as long as normal. Gillie thanked us all for our hard work and for sharing what had been our private thoughts. She finished by saying, "If anyone feels that they need to talk in private about anything discussed this afternoon, my door is always open."

We all thanked her and left. She is such a lovely person. We are so fortunate to have a staff member who is so open and understanding.

As I was walking away from the Music Block, Simon hurriedly joined me and said hesitantly, "Amanda, you were very brave sharing the story of your bullying with us. Thank you. It must have taken a lot of effort. What happened in there, you won't mention it to anyone, will you?"

I replied, "Of course I won't. Your secret is safe with me."

He then really surprised me by saying, "I have an idea which I'd like to share with you. I'll tell you about it after dinner tomorrow. Would you mind if I borrowed a copy of your song words?"

I replied, "That's fine, as long as you don't show them to anyone else."

"No, of course I won't. See you," he said as he left.

What an eventful afternoon! I felt I could trust him and I rushed off to share the news of the afternoon with Immie. Of course, I didn't tell her everything as I had made a promise to Simon and the rest of the group.

Memories and mixed emotions!
Love, Amanda

Term 1 Entry 17

Dear H,

The evening of the Song Writing session, Immie had sat spellbound whilst I told her about what had happened that afternoon. However, I was careful not to share any of the personal stories that I had heard. She kept asking me questions about Simon that seemed to be so absurd that I couldn't answer them.

She came to the conclusion that Simon wanted to ask me out on a date. "But he's older than me and why would he want a copy of my song words?"

"That's just an excuse," laughed Immie.

Neither of us could wait to see what Simon had planned for the following evening. I had butterflies in my stomach just like I'd experienced when I'd had to sing before I came to the Academy. I must admit I couldn't think of much else that day, which is not like me at all.

I insisted that Immie stick by my side like glue during dinner. I need not have worried as she had no intention of not being in on the action. She was as excited as I was, if not, even more so.

After we had finished eating, Simon arrived clutching a guitar case. He suggested that we go into one of the practise rooms in the Block and that Immie was welcome to join us if I agreed. Of course, she didn't hold back. In fact, I thought I saw her fluttering her eyelashes. I nudged her and mouthed, "Stop it!"

Simon sat down to play his guitar and he began to sing. He admitted that the song was meant to be sung by me, but he just wanted us to listen and tell us what we thought. I have never been so speechless. The tune was so beautiful. He had based his tune on the tune I had sung when I had shared 'The Daisy Chain' with the class, but had added extra features. As I was so taken aback, I couldn't stop the tears from rolling down my cheeks. Simon said, "You don't like it do you? Tell me the truth."

I stammered, "No, it's not that! The tune is just perfect. I never expected it to sound so beautiful. Thank you. No one has ever done anything like this for me before."

Immie sat there and just kept saying, "Wow, wow. It's so cool. Now you sing it Amanda whilst Simon plays."

After I'd sung it a few times and Simon had added a few more chords to the background, we were satisfied that we'd done the best we could for the evening. Simon suggested we perform the song together at the next Song Writing session. I thanked him again and Immie and I left him practising for his lesson with his tutor.

It was a great evening. Simon was another friend I'd made. Even though Immie kept suggesting there was more to it and teased me endlessly. I told her I felt the same as her and that, as I also wanted to eventually study singing overseas, I wasn't looking for a boyfriend, but a 'boy friend' would be just fine, especially one as cute looking as Simon!

Life is full of surprises!

Amanda

Term 1 Entry 18

Dear H,

I've just spoken to Immie. She arrived at my door, dreadfully upset and angry. It's the first time I've seen her like this. She'd just returned from the first orchestral rehearsal for our big end of semester concert. She had been chosen to play the piano with the whole orchestra for the first half of the concert. It was a huge responsibility and a great honour.

"I left all my music in the correct order in a file on the piano," she said adamantly. When she had sat down to play, the conductor became so angry with her when she couldn't find the music in the correct order. She realised that it had been tampered with and that the sheets of music had been rearranged into a shuffled mess. She said she'd been horrified and so embarrassed. As a result, she had to keep everyone waiting whilst she sorted the music out. Jessica, in particular, was outspoken and after huffing and puffing in 'so called' exaggeration, said loudly, "I told you, you weren't up to it."

Immie had apologised to the conductor, a prestigious visiting Professor of Music. He sternly replied, in no uncertain terms, "There is no room in my orchestra for someone who cannot organise their music! I will give you one more chance."

Under her breath, Jessica was heard to say, "If I were you, I wouldn't. She's not worth it."

Afterwards, Immie told me she had heard exactly what Jessica had said; neither had she missed the raised eyebrows and joyful innocence written across her smug face. Although Jessica is no doubt an excellent pianist, she has an inflated opinion of her musical talent and doesn't appear to be able to cope with anyone who she sees as being a threat to her ego. It was quite obvious who had shuffled the music around, but it would be very difficult to prove. Immie told me she would not let her music out of her sight in future and she would try hard not to let Jessica's comments get to her. I was surprised when Immie confided in me, that there had been other occasions when Jessica had tried to make her look foolish in front of other people and that was not all! Immie hinted at cyber bullying but didn't want to discuss this any further.

"Come on, what we need is a bike ride!" I suggested.

Thoughts churning,
Wheels turning,
Anger burning!

Body shaking,
Heart quaking,
Muscles aching.

Downhill speeding,
Tension easing,
Stress releasing!

Always there for you,

Amanda

Term 2 Entry 1

Dear H,

It's now Term Two and I've just returned to the Academy after the Autumn two week break. How times flies! It's hard to believe that I'm no longer a new girl. I spent the two weeks at home. Mum took a few days off work to spend with me. Remember last year how I spent so much time alone after I returned home from school every evening? Thankfully, times have changed for the better. It's beginning to seem like a distant dream.

Mum treated me to a trip to see Philippe her award winning hairstylist. Can you remember the first time he styled my hair? He really scared me as he cut it so very short. I had bravely made an appointment midterm at the local hairstylists, close to the Academy. There, the stylist trimmed it, and although she tried her best, she didn't seem to have the knack with my hair that Philippe has. I was hanging out to see him. He was as thrilled to see me as I was to see him. He commented how slim and healthy I appeared and asked me loads of questions about life at the Academy. Each time I answered him, he replied, "Awesome!"

Mum also treated me to some new clothes. She couldn't believe how much taller I'd grown in three months. One of the BEST things was to go for some fittings for my Concert dress. We all have to wear a dress made from the same shimmery royal blue fabric but can choose our own design. However, the design has to be passed as suitable by the Academy. Mum arranged for a designer, who she works with, to design a dress especially for me. The design was scanned and emailed to the Academy who passed it as suitable. I'm so lucky having a mother in the fashion industry. The dress fits superbly and it has an underskirt in pale blue taffeta which rustles as I walk and holds the flared skirt in position. I wish you could see it. It has a boat shaped neck, small cap sleeves which are slightly gathered and is fitting until the hip line when the skirt flares out.

I was also treated to a new pair of glittery silver shoes with a kitten heel. Mum explained to me that because I wasn't used to wearing high heels it would be better for me to have a lower heel and then I'd be balanced as I walked to the microphone for my solos. She said, "We don't want you wobbling about do we?"

Mum explained that walking in a long dress with layers of fabric required some style and that I was to take smaller steps, walk slower and hold myself up tall. She then demonstrated. It was really funny as she got a bit carried away and started to show me how NOT to walk before she demonstrated on HOW to walk properly. I never realised how silly Mum can act until recently. She can be really funny. I've been practising walking in the dress with the shoes on. It's amazing how wearing a sophisticated dress makes you feel so different and SO grown up! I feel absolutely thrilled with it and can't wait until the night of the concert. I AM SO LUCKY!

Whilst I was at home, I brought out my old bike and cycled to visit Mrs Field, my first singing teacher. She wanted to know all of the details of how I was getting on and, of course, she wanted to hear me sing. I told her all about the Song Writing Option and about my success with my song, 'The Daisy Chain' and all about Simon's musical arrangement.

I saw a lot of Emma. She's really cool. She's accepted that she has a permanent injury and will not walk again, but this doesn't mean that she's content to sit and feel sorry for herself. Since I first met her, she has really 'come out of her shell' in a big way. She's becoming quite a rebel. She joins in with everything that she is physically capable of doing.

This year she has become heavily involved in wheelchair sports, especially basketball. I haven't watched her in action yet, but I can imagine her as an impressive player on court. She has such a strong, assertive personality. She's really great. It can't be easy for her.

She still sings and is very passionate about it. She's also good at TALKING and always fills me in with all the latest gossip, especially news concerning Cassandra, even though I'd rather not hear about her.

Emma told me that St Ursula's had started a Daisy Chain group. I wonder what lead them to do that!! Not soon enough I thought to myself. How I would have benefitted from such a group when I'd been there. Although, I'm not sure back then that I would have had the courage to have joined. I'm seriously thinking of starting up a group at St C's, especially after the episode with Jessica.

The two weeks break passed by so quickly. I must admit, I did find home a bit on the quiet side, especially when Mum and Dad were at work. I missed the fact that there is always someone to talk to here at St C's, especially Immie. However, I did enjoy being able to stay in bed later in the mornings and catch up on my 'beauty sleep'. Life is SO full on at the Academy that it's good to take time out to relax.

At times, having lots of girls living on the same corridor can be a pain, especially when you can hear lots of giggles, (occasionally hysterics!), loud laughter and music beating from one end of the corridor to the other. Sometimes, when you've oodles of school work to do and you are trying to concentrate, you feel like screaming, but that's not often.

We can't be perfect all of the time!
Yours, Amanda

Term 2 Entry 2

Dear H,

I've just received an email from Emma. It's really important so I must share it with you. She says her school is full of the latest rumours concerning Cassandra. It appears Cassandra is HEADLINE NEWS, but not for good reasons! Was she ever? Quite a few of the girls at Emma's school are friendly with students from St Ursula's so bad news travels even faster than good news. It appears Cassandra has really overstepped the mark this time. It's about time she was caught out.

Well, here's the latest! A few of the teachers and some of the parents of students at St Ursula's had received anonymous phone calls in the middle of the night. Each call was muffled but the messages were clear enough and they weren't pleasant. Each call was accompanied by lots of giggling in the background. No one knew who had made the calls as they were made by using a landline and the message on the phone screen always said, 'Anonymous, Private Number'.

Other staff members were complaining of receiving inappropriate messages on Social Media from someone calling themselves, Samantha Truble, who ended all of her messages with the words, 'Bite Back'.

No one suspected Cassandra who announced with great

importance, so that everyone could hear, that her mum had also received a call and how appalling it was to be woken in the middle of the night. She also added that her mother had mentioned about some awful messages she had received on her Facebook page and how disgusting it was.

The following week, there was a repeat of the performance with calls being made to some staff members at Cranfield High, Emma's school, as well as calls made to other staff members at St Ursula's. No one was pleased about the calls; in fact some people were livid and had phoned the police and had arranged with their phone companies to put a trace on their lines. However, on this occasion, the caller, Samantha, was growing more confident by the minute as she obviously imagined she could get away with the offences. She boldly asked one member of staff at St Ursula's if they would accept a Reverse Charge call, and before thinking what she was doing, had accidently given her real name. Guess who it turned out to be? It certainly wasn't Samantha. It was CASSANDRA!!

Waiting expectantly!
Amanda

Term 2 Entry 3

Dear H,

I've just Skyped Mum. You will NEVER guess what she had to tell me! Last night, she had just returned from work when Cassandra's Mum, Annabelle, appeared at the front door in a terrible state. She's normally so well dressed with immaculate long blond hair and make-up, in fact, an older version of Cassandra. You can't say that she's Mum's 'best friend'.

Mum did at one time see her quite often socially. Remember, the fashion parade and the awful lunch party that mum organised and insisted that Cassandra attend with her mother? Well, since the day I opened up and confided about the bullying I had received from Cassandra and her gang, Mum was so disgusted and had tried to avoid seeing Cassandra's mother. It probably wasn't fair to take it out on Cassandra's mum as she hadn't been aware that her daughter had been behaving so atrociously. Mum said that she felt she didn't want to have to hear anymore about Cassandra and so it was better not to have contact with her mother. However, when Annabelle arrived at the door, looking so dishevelled with mascara running down her face, Mum said she felt she couldn't slam the door in her face.

Mum continued with the story. She said that Dad had then appeared at the front door clutching a pile of work files in one hand and his glasses in the other. He was inquisitive to see what the commotion was all about AND TO MAKE SURE that Mum was safe. Mum nodded her head to indicate to him that perhaps it was a good idea for her to deal with the situation and mouthed to him, "Women's Business" so he'd understand.

She led Annabelle, tottering unsteadily on her 'mock tiger skin' platform stilettos, into the kitchen where she suggested she sat down at the breakfast bar and where she quickly pushed a cup of coffee towards her. THEN SHE LISTENED TO THE STORY IN AMAZEMENT!! Annabelle spluttered between her gulps of coffee and tears, "I received a call whilst I was at work... It was Mrs Pringle, you know, the school's Headmistress. She didn't ask politely, but insisted that I go directly to the school. I told her I was at the office and had a client with me and that I couldn't just drop everything unless it was a matter of great urgency."

Mrs Pringle had replied, "It certainly isn't a social call. I need you here NOW. I have some very unpleasant news to impart to you concerning your daughter. The sooner you come, the better!"

"Well, I didn't know what to think. At first, I was concerned that something had happened to Cassandra, so I grabbed my bag and ran towards the car park. I'm ashamed to say, I left the client sitting there."

When she arrived at the school, Cassandra's mother was told, in no uncertain terms, about the phone calls and Facebook messages from 'Bite Back'. At first, she insisted that Cassandra would never do such things and that her beloved daughter was CERTAINLY NOT 'BITE BACK'! THEN Cassandra was led into the office sobbing hysterically and, WAIT FOR IT, she ADMITTED that she had made all of the calls from the home landline but she wouldn't admit to the writing of the unsavoury messages on Facebook.

"I wouldn't do a thing like that. I don't have a Facebook account!" she exploded through her tears.

The Headmistress of the school made it very clear that St Ursula's would not tolerate such behaviour and the decision had been to expel Cassandra that very day. In fact, they had made Cassandra pack up all of her books in readiness to take them home with her.

Mum told me that Annabelle had felt so embarrassed and humiliated that she couldn't stop shaking and that she had hardly the strength to stand. However, she had found some hidden strength from somewhere and had forced herself to 'frog-march' Cassandra out of the Headmistress's office, through the main entrance, down the school steps and into the car park where she had bundled Cassandra into her car. Annabelle said she was in such a rage she didn't know how she contained herself.

When she arrived home, there was a message on the answering machine from the client who she had deserted in the office earlier that afternoon. The message, informed her that the contract she was planning to sign in the office had been cancelled and that the client was transferring her business elsewhere. It wasn't a day that Annabelle felt she could celebrate.

By this time, Cassandra's mum had begun to sob hysterically and Mum admitted that she didn't know what to do or say to her so she pushed a box of tissues towards her, pressed the button on the coffee machine and waited for the second cup of coffee. When Annabelle finally managed to calm herself down, Mum led her to the door, Annabelle turned round and said, "Thank you so much for sparing the time to listen to me. I haven't the courage to talk to anyone else. I thought that the people who Cassandra phoned were my friends, but they are now refusing to speak to me. My whole world has collapsed and I don't know what to do."

I can't believe it. After all this time, Cassandra has been found out. I must tell Emma, but firstly she must promise to keep it a secret.

I can't believe it!

Love, Amanda

Term 2 Entry 4

Dear H,

I thought I'd keep you up to date with my sporting activities!
I really enjoyed Cycling last term and I'll continue doing it as
there's a group who go cycling early in the morning. It means
I have to get up extra early. It's often an effort to get up
that early, but I think it's worth it. That's the plan. We'll
have to wait and see if I can keep to it!

This term, I've decided to give Yoga a try. I think it'll help me
relax. There's a meditation session at the end, so I'll see how
I go with that. There's so much talk at present about being
Mindful. It appears, Yoga helps you to become Mindful. Have
you heard of the term? I believe it means just being in the
present and concentrating on what is happening at that
moment. It certainly sounds a good idea. I'm looking forward
to giving it a try. I'll let you know how it works.

I must go. Lots to do.

Amanda

Term 2 Entry 5

Dear H,
I'M NOT IN A GOOD MOOD! Why? Don't even think of asking!

Everyone, well perhaps an exaggeration, but it seems like
everyone is talking about the amount of free time that
Immie and Simon are spending together. They appear to be
sneaking off to the Block after lessons and they are both
tight-lipped about it. It's not like Immie to be so secretive.
She's still friendly towards me but she is avoiding replying to
my questions about her visits to the Block.

"You'll just have to wait and see," she replied mysteriously.

I can't understand why, but it's really making me cross. Why
are they being so mysterious? I don't handle secrets well. I
suppose it's due to past history. It makes me feel suspicious
and that whatever is happening behind my back isn't a good
thing. Then, to make matters worse, certain girls, one being
Jessica, are starting to say hurtful things like, "We thought
you and Simon were an item. Did he dump you?"

I must admit, I'm feeling disappointed. Simon was never my
boyfriend but I thought he was a special friend who I could
trust and confide in.

I'm really surprised by how I feel about Simon. It doesn't appear logical. There's no real reason why I should feel this way. It's not as though I'm jealous of Immie. Is it? NO IT ISN'T!

I thought this school would be different. That I'd finished with all of the bullying but now, I'm not so sure. I'm feeling really dejected.

Anyway, I'll do what I've always done and just carry on regardless. I've had enough practice.

Life wasn't meant to be easy.

Amanda

PS I've just passed Tilly in the corridor. She doesn't look very well. Says she's picked up a stomach bug. Hope it's not catching.

Term 2 Entry 6

Dear H,

I rang Gran last night and told her all that had been happening. I opened up my heart and my recent feelings of insecurity and lack of trust came pouring out in flood-like proportions. The whole story, about Immie and Simon disappearing and spending time together, had affected me far more than I'd imagined. I thought I'd completely recovered from my emotional rollercoaster that I'd experienced prior to arriving at St C's, but it doesn't appear to be so. I suppose after all I went through at St Ursula's, it's bound to have left a lasting impression. However, my fabulous Gran has invited me to stay with her this coming weekend!! Yippee!

"You do sound rather down in the dumps for a girl with a birthday coming up this weekend," she stated. "I had planned to invite you for the weekend but didn't mention it as I thought you'd prefer to spend it celebrating with your new friends instead of with an old lady like me."

"Oh no!" I replied enthusiastically, "I'd love to spend the weekend with you. We always have such fun."

"OK, you'd better go and clear it with Ms Longhirst and make sure it's OK with your Mum," she said. "Let me know your plans and I'll arrange to collect you."

It's great that Gran lives within commuting distance. It's my fourteenth birthday on Sunday. I expect you seem rather surprised?

I raced off along the corridor to speak to Gillie. She answered with, "I'm pleased to see you looking happy. I've been worried about you. I noticed you've been looking rather miserable just lately. Is there anything bothering you? You would tell me if anything was wrong wouldn't you?"

Before I'd had the chance to answer, she continued with, "Oh, isn't it your birthday this weekend?"

"Yes... it is my birthday but I don't want anyone to know about it. I'm fine. Just a bit tired. I just need a couple of days with Gran. That'll do the trick."

She agreed that a short break would do me good but I think she thought I was being a bit strange. No one here knows it's my birthday. I don't want to make a big thing about it. You know what I think about parties and surprises.

Well Mum has given her permission so I'd better contact Gran. I suppose I ought to do my homework before I go away although I'm not over enthusiastic about it.

Feeling more sparkly, Amanda

PS I've just seen Immie in the corridor and announced that I'm going away for the weekend. She raised her eyebrows in surprise and then sighed heavily in disappointment. She said, "Oh, Simon and I have a surprise for you but it will have to wait now until next week. What a shame! Have a good time."

I wonder what that's all about? I've given up trying to work out what is happening in other people's minds.

Term 2 Entry 7

Dear H,

I've just returned to St C's after having had a terrific time with Gran... dinner AND a theatre trip on the Saturday. We also managed to fit in some serious shopping on the Saturday afternoon! It was actually my birthday on the Sunday but I had to travel back to the Academy early on Sunday afternoon. Mum and Dad phoned to wish me a Happy Birthday first thing in the morning and Mum announced that she was arranging something special, as a birthday celebration, for me during the next school holiday when I'm home. I really hope it's not one of her themed events! Fingers crossed!

Gran is really awesome and seems to know just what to say to help me feel better. The good thing about her is that she NEVER tells me what to do. She listens whilst I talk and talk until I've got everything out of my system and then she asks me questions and somehow, by answering the questions, I have the answers to my problems. After I've chatted to her and opened up my heart and let all of my problems tumble out, I feel as though the tension has lifted and been spirited away. My thoughts become less chaotic and I can see so much clearer. I feel my self-esteem rising and I generally feel more confident and ready to take on the world.

I am so fortunate to have Gran as my confidant. I feel that

I can talk to her about anything. Do you have someone in your life like that? I really don't know what I'd do without her. I don't even want to think about it. It's too terrifying. I remember what it was like when I used to return home from St Ursula's and Mum was far too busy engrossed in her business to talk to me, and listening to me, was quite out of the equation. Thankfully, that's all changed for the better. I even get the odd mumble now from Dad when I phone home.

No more tears
In the deep dark night
When despair is at its worst
And the black dog comes to bite.

No more tears.
No more tears.

Well, getting side tracked again! I must stop doing it.

I forgot to tell you, Gran treated me to see 'Matilda, the Musical'. It was amazing and so dynamic. It blew me away to another world. Most of the performers were so young, but oh so talented. Every time I see a stage show, I am even more convinced that the only thing I want to do is to follow a singing career on the stage. I love some of the songs and must ask Mrs Blake if I can include them in my vocal lessons. Follow your dreams!, Amanda

Term 2 Entry 8

Dear H,

Rumours are swirling around like smoke rings. Once one ring has wafted away, there's another rising in close pursuit. The senior girls are the worst offenders. They always seem to be discussing 'Top Secrets' in hushed tones. If you happen to walk in their direction, they instantly stop talking and stare at you as if you have committed a crime. They make you feel very uncomfortable and you feel as though you'd like to be whisked far away. Jessica is always on the scene trying to muscle her way into the centre of the smoke ring. The 'Top Secrets' of the latest smoke ring are filtering down to the younger girls and I hope, what I've heard, isn't true.

Well, since I've returned, everyone on our floor is so busy with the gossip that concerns Tilly that I don't think anyone realised that I'd been away. That was good from my point of view, as I was secretly dreading any further comments about Simon and Immie.

The latest rumour is that Tilly is still not at all well. Her best friend, Amy, insists that Tilly is just suffering from some stomach bug. She explained that Tilly ate something at the local cafe when she met Jacques and ever since then, she's not felt well. She certainly doesn't look her normal bouncy self. She's still very pale and gives the impression of being anxious as though she has the weight of the world on her shoulders. Now I think about it, I haven't seen her in the block for ages. I hope she's OK. She's a brilliant flautist with a really bright future ahead of her.

It's time for me to unpack and prepare for tomorrow. I have some homework I need to catch up on.

Amanda

Term 2 Entry 9

Dear H,

I'd only been in my room for a few minutes last evening when Immie knocked on the door. She appeared to be rather self-conscious and not her normal confident self. She asked, "Did you have a good weekend?" and followed by, "I missed you."

"Yes, it was fab," I replied unemotionally and not giving much away.

When I failed to share anymore information with her, she asked, "Do you have some spare time this evening?"

I tentatively replied, "Yes. I think I can fit in a short time after dinner."

I was still feeling stung by her recent secrecy but the feelings had weakened somewhat over the weekend and were not quite so intense. I had discussed with Gran how I'd felt about the situation regarding Immie and Simon's strange behaviour. She had hesitantly suggested that there may be a perfectly reasonable explanation for their actions. She didn't mention anything about me over reacting but I sensed that she thought I had taken everything far too seriously. I suppose old habits are hard to break. When you've experienced bullying, it's sometimes hard to trust people and sometimes, even small things can tip you over.

After dinner, Immie and Simon appeared together and said
they had a surprise for me but I had to walk to the block
with them. It was a dark and chilly evening and I thought to
myself that this had better be good. When we arrived and
entered one of the rooms which had a piano in, I noticed
Simon's guitar leaning against a chair.

"Sit down and close your eyes and listen," said Simon.

So I did as they asked. It wasn't long before I had hot tears
streaming down my face. What I heard was magical and took
my breath away. What a fool I had been! Simon and Immie
had been spending their spare time working on a professional
musical arrangement for my song, 'The Daisy Chain'. The
second time, Simon played and sang the song and Immie joined
him on the piano. When they had finished, he said, "Dry your
eyes, Amanda, and you sing this time round. I don't know
what the matter is; girls always seem to be crying."

That started me off more than ever. Immie enveloped me
in a huge hug and whispered in my ear, "Happy Birthday. We
were so disappointed you weren't here over the weekend. We
wanted to give you a birthday surprise."

I realised I had been worrying needlessly. My mind had gone
into overdrive with my spiralling thoughts taking control.
All of my fears instantly melted away and I was a blubbering

mess. Could I sing that evening? The answer was, NO. After the tears had subsided, I began to feel stupid and that my reaction had been over the top. I tried to explain that I wasn't used to such kindness from friends but asked them never to do anything as a secret again. I didn't want to mention the gossip that had emerged from them disappearing off together but I think Immie understood.

Simon, being a male, probably had no idea. Hopefully, he'll remain in ignorance. I later admitted to Immie that it had been a marvellous birthday present.

"Why didn't you mention anything about your birthday? We knew it was sometime around now. I collected the mail and saw all the envelopes addressed to you," Immie mentioned.

"I didn't want a fuss," I explained.

"Amanda, you are SO annoying at times," she replied with a huge grin on her face.

We agreed that we'd return the following evening so I could sing my song with the new musical arrangement and iron out any problems with the music. For my part, I was thrilled with the accompaniment and thought it was perfect.

Over the moon... and back!, Amanda

Term 2 Entry 10

Dear H,

I'm still feeling emotional, a bit up and down. However, I realise now that I over reacted to the Simon/Immie situation. I spent so long at my previous school feeling the 'odd-one-out'. Since then, my life has changed dramatically but every so often, I feel the old anxieties rising from the pit of my stomach. Most of the time, I feel so grown up and able to cope and being confident is not a problem. Then, every so often, the child inside me appears and all the confidence melts away. It's hard being a teen isn't it? You're neither an adult nor a child.

It really touched me that two new friends had taken the time to do something so special as to arrange the music for my song. I shouldn't have been so suspicious. To anyone else, it may not have been a 'big' thing, but to me, unused to such kindness from friends, it was 'huge'. I tried to explain to Immie, and apologised for doubting her friendship, but she gave me a big hug and told me not to be so silly and forget all about it.

Silly Me!

Amanda

Term 2 Entry 11

Dear H,

Well, reading this, you would think that we don't actually do any serious work here. The teachers seem to be happy with my grades for my academic work. I won't bore you with all of the details.

My Vocal Studies are progressing really well. My 'very' favourite time is when I sing. It is MY special time. When I sing, I feel myself carried away to another place and time, somewhere where only I can go. No one else can reach me. The feeling is SO fulfilling. I can't explain it any better than that.

I'm also finding my Sports Option, Yoga, is really helping with my singing. There are certain positions, one where we stretch into something that makes us all look as though we are bananas. I can't remember what it's called but it is excellent at opening up our diaphragms. I feel much freer inside and my voice has more strength after I've practised the position.

The meditation is also having benefits, although I don't find it easy. I've just got the worst mind for meditation! It tends to wander all over the place. If I'm not careful, it doesn't just wander, it whizzes!! Do you know what I mean? The instructor says that doesn't matter, just let the thought go and return to concentrating on the image being used in the lesson. I don't think the instructor would be impressed if I told her that a lot of my ideas for Song Writing crop up whilst I'm supposed to be meditating!! Oops!

I find the breathing techniques are really good for me. You can't think of much else when you are busy counting your breaths. My favourite is where we breathe in for four counts, hold our breath for seven counts and breathe out slowly over a count of eight. I sometimes repeat this a few times if I feel I need to relax. Another exercise is where a series of body parts are named one after the other. Our job is to concentrate just on the part named and try not to think of anything else. I suppose I'm more of a success at being Mindful with this exercise!!

Everyone in the class agrees that after a yoga session they feel more relaxed so we must be doing something right.

Close your eyes.
Picture a daisy
Its face pointing towards the sun.
Watered by the rain,
Standing firm,
Tall and proud.
Is that you?

Walking on air!
From a relaxed Amanda

Term 2 Entry 12

Dear H,
I've just had a VERY long talk to Mum on Skype.

Well, Mum was telling me that she was shopping in the local supermarket earlier in the day when she literally bumped into Cassandra's mum, Annabelle. She told me that this time Annabelle was her usual model-like self, her face was made-up perfectly and there wasn't a hair on her head that was out of place. However, she noticed that Annabelle didn't appear to be her normal confident self. Her sparkle was missing. Mum felt that something wasn't quite right. As I mentioned before, Annabelle, is not one of Mum's best friends. However, when she asked Mum if she had time to go for a coffee, Mum hesitantly replied, "I can give you half an hour."

Mum still can't forget how Cassandra bullied me at St Ursula's. However, she told me that she remembered the time when Annabelle had unexpectedly turned up at the house and how she had told Mum she had lost all of her friends due to Cassandra's phone and Facebook antics. I suppose Mum feels sorry for her.

This is where the story begins to become more interesting. Cassandra is still living with her mother and attending a local school in the city. However, things are far from perfect.

Cassandra visits her father and his new wife on alternate weekends. She confided in Mum that when Cassandra was much younger, Dominic, her father, had idolised her. She had been 'Daddy's little Princess'. In his eyes, Cassandra was prettier, more talented, and more intelligent than everyone else, and so the list had gone on. When the marriage had broken up and Dominic had left, this was when the problems had begun.

Annabelle continued, "I never realised the effect of him leaving must have had on Cassandra. I was so full up with my own emotions at the time. She must have felt so unimportant. Her world must have shattered around her in tiny fragments."

Annabelle admitted that she had found the breakup hard. She told Mum that as a girl, she had come from a poor background where there had been few opportunities. She had met Dominic at a party, and after a whirlwind romance, he had proposed and she had readily accepted. Marriage followed soon after. Dominic was rich, handsome and was everything she thought she wanted in life. However, she also had dreams to do something with her life and had gone ahead and started up her own business importing designer shoes.

At first, it had just been a small business, more like a hobby, which she had run from the spare room at home. Much to her surprise, the business had steadily grown in strength, and had led to Annabelle opening a huge warehouse for her stock and employing staff to deal with the ever increasing orders. However, following her dream, had taken up all of her time. Annabelle admitted that Dominic and Cassandra had been left for long periods of time whilst she had climbed the ladder of fame and fortune. As a result, Cassandra had often stayed overnight at the homes of her friends whilst Annabelle had attended business meetings and fashion events late into the night.

At these times, Dominic had begun to spend time with his secretary, a widow with two young children. Annabelle, by now with tears streaming down her cheeks, stated that it was obvious to her why Dominic had strayed and begun to show far more interest in his secretary, who was willing to put him first.

"I must admit, thinking back to that time, that neither of us gave Cassandra much thought. When we decided to separate, we were too involved with our own emotions," she sniffed between the tears.

By now, the half hour that Mum had agreed to listen to Annabelle was fast approaching an hour. Mum realised that Annabelle desperately needed to confide in someone, and as her friends had deserted her, Mum felt obliged to sit and listen. She was quite startled when Annabelle suddenly came to the realisation and stated, "You know, I never gave it a thought until now, but Cassandra must have missed the attention dreadfully that Dominic used to lavish upon her so much."

Like a lightning bolt she continued, "This must have been why Cassandra rebelled!"

At first Mum admitted to me that she found it hard to believe that Annabelle had been so unaware of Cassandra's needs, but then she said her mind had wandered back to her own situation. It was not until Emma had presented me with the silver daisy chain, that Mum researched its significance and found out it was the symbol for an anti-bullying group. Until that time, she had absolutely no idea that I had been bullied so intensely at St Ursula's.

Mum said she quickly switched her thoughts back to Annabelle and tuned her mind into listening fully to the story. Annabelle continued along the theme, "The divorce must have been Cassandra's worst nightmare. We should have considered her more. It's no wonder her behaviour deteriorated. She probably felt that she had to blame someone for this new situation she found herself in. No wonder she began the bullying. It must have made her feel important."

Mum said she ordered another coffee and wondered how much

longer the conversation was going to carry on.

Annabelle continued, "How alone and unhappy she must have felt! If only I'd thought about her, instead of myself. She must have felt we'd deserted her. All of this recent behaviour must be a kind of pay back."

She continued on with the saga and related how Dominic had gone ahead, after the divorce, and married his secretary, Sophie. Annabelle then described an incident a few weeks ago when Cassandra had returned home from a weekend with her Dad and his new family. When Annabelle had asked her if she'd had a good time she'd stated brusquely, "Dad thinks those girls are perfect in every way. It makes me SICK! They never do a thing wrong. I HATE them!"

She had then stormed into her room and had banged the door shut. Through the closed door, Annabelle heard her throwing things around and ranting, "It's not fair, not fair! Why should they be happy when I'm not? Just wait until next time. Then they'll know what it's like to feel pain."

Annabelle shuddered with the thought of it, "I do hope she's not planning on doing something stupid. I should have gone in to talk to her, asked her to explain and not just left her to cry herself to sleep. You must think I'm dreadful! "

By this time, Mum explained that she really did have a pressing appointment and that she hoped everything would sort itself out. "We all make mistakes," she said on leaving Annabelle. "I'll phone you later this evening and make sure you're alright."

"I'll be fine. I really want to thank you for giving up your time and listening to me. I really appreciate it."

Before Mum finished relating the story to me, she said, "Amanda, I am so pleased that we managed to become closer. Annabelle's story of Cassandra reminds me of how little time I used to spend with you and how my business took over. I'm so sorry."

"It's OK Mum. It's a thing of the past. Love you Mum."

"I love you too," she replied.

It's so true. My story could have had an unhappy ending. Thanks to Emma and Gran, my Fairy Godmother, my life is back on track and my fractured relationship with Mum is a thing of the past.

Feeling loved,

Amanda

Term 2 Entry 13

Dear H,

I can't believe how the time is flying by. Rehearsals are now in full swing for our end of Semester Concert and I have some great news. Simon, Immie and I were rehearsing my song, 'The Daisy Chain'. Gillie heard us and asked us to perform the song at the concert. We were so thrilled to be asked and are so excited. I'm keeping it as a surprise for Mum, Dad and Gran but I have shared the news with Emma and made her promise not to breathe a word to anyone. I can tell you that isn't going to be easy for her!

Everyone is in a state of excitement as we are all given the chance to perform in our chosen area of music. Unfortunately, not everyone can perform a solo. I'm singing two solos as well as 'The Daisy Chain' and I'm also singing with the choir. Phew!

I can't believe what an effect the concert is having on people. It's weird. The nicest people have become so competitive. Everyone seems to think they are better than anyone else and we are all living on a 'knife edge'. It's all ridiculous. But as I've found out, performers often have big egos.

Jessica is a real prima donna. She just can't bear the thought that someone may play the piano as well, if not better than her, especially if that person is younger. She is forever, finding fault with Immie's piano performances. Her actions have became more and more obvious especially when she found out that Immie had been chosen to accompany the orchestra, and play two pieces of music, and she only had one. So far Immie has kept very calm and has not let Jessica see how upset she has been. However, I have seen some of the tricks Jessica has been playing.

I'm sure there are other students who are also being bullied but who are not saying anything. Next time I have a chance to talk to Gillie, I will suggest that we start a Daisy Chain group at St C's.

Changing the subject, did I mention that we can also wear a purple silk flower with our dresses? Some girls are wearing them as a hair decoration or attached to a headband. Some are wearing them on a belt at the waist, and some are wearing them as a corsage. I'm not sure what I'm going to do with mine yet. I'm hoping Mum will come up with the right answer. I can't wait to see everyone. It'll be awesome.

From a very excited,
Amanda

Term 2 Entry 14

Dear H,

As I mentioned before, all our energy is presently geared towards the concert and we are all under tremendous pressure. The music tutors keep reminding us about 'perfection'. I wish they wouldn't as it only makes me tenser. Everyone is walking around looking as though they are carrying great weights on their shoulders. We are all so serious and no one appears to find anything amusing. It's gross.

Thankfully, I'm finding the Yoga classes useful. The breathing techniques are really helping me with my singing, and the meditation at the end of the session, is something I can practise on my own when things get a bit too much! I am improving with my technique of being Mindful, well, I'm trying!

School work continues as usual. We still have to keep up with that and sometimes the amount of work is a pain as I'd rather be putting the effort into my music. However, that's not how it works.

I understand that Tilly is still sick and trying to hide it from everyone. She's still saying, she has a stomach bug and is refusing adamantly to go to the Dr in the Academy Sick Bay. She looks terribly unhappy and worried. I've heard that she is still seeing Jacques but according to the gossip, things appear to be strained between them. People say they have seen them arguing. I suppose it will sort itself out.

I nearly forgot to tell you. I mentioned to Gillie that I had concerns about bullying. She surprised me by saying, "I've heard a few rumours myself. How about we have a chat about forming a Daisy Chain group?"

"Great!" I replied, "I'll contact my friend Emma and see if she has any ideas on the best way of setting one up."

I can't wait to speak to Emma about it.

So much to do!

Amanda

Term 2 Entry 15

Dear H,

Wow! I'm really excited. Simon has offered to teach me some chords on the guitar. He says it'll help me with my song writing. That will start some new gossip. I really like Simon. What have I just written! I must remind myself that I'm not looking for a boyfriend! However, if you saw him, he's really cool, tall with blonde hair and the bluest of eyes, you'd realise a girl would be mad not to be flattered by his friendship. I sometimes wonder if he has a girlfriend at home that he's keeping a secret.

Stop day dreaming!

Amanda

Term 2 Entry 16

Dear H,

Time is running away with all of us. Everyday seems to have fewer hours than the day before... if that's possible. Not long now until the concert. Everyone appears to be getting more anxious and stressed out than before. It's all this niggling rivalry that is getting on my nerves. I just don't get it. Here at St C's, we are all good at our chosen music speciality, otherwise we wouldn't have been selected to attend the Academy, so why does everyone persistently aim to be seen as better than anyone else? It's just not in my nature to be like that and I know that Immie feels the same way.

However, in the middle of my 'flat-out' schedule, don't forget we still have our school work to keep up with. I did manage to fit in a Skype session with Emma and asked her if she could supply me with any information on the setting up of a Daisy Chain group. She was the one who originally introduced me to the idea of a Daisy Chain and since they've set one up at my previous school, St Ursula's, I thought she'd be the obvious choice. Emma, my first and very best friend, didn't disappoint me. She's agreed to do some research and email me some information.

I also phoned Gran and had a chat with her about it. She said, "I think what you are proposing to do is marvellous Amanda.

I'll give it some thought and see if I can come up with any useful information. The more information you have, the better."

I'll let Gillie know and then we can have a get together when we have more information. I don't know how it's going to work or whether it will work but I've got to do something.

I am beginning to notice the impact that Jessica is having on Immie and I don't like it. Immie, who is normally so in control of herself, is actually beginning to believe some of the things that Jessica is saying to her and her confidence is taking a battering. I keep having to have chats with her to remind her how brilliant she really is. I can't let this continue. I know how desperate I was when I was the victim of bullying.

I'll keep you posted. I must go to catch up with some school work.

Until next time,
Amanda

Term 2 Entry 17

Dear H,

I just had to share this news with you. Mum texted me yesterday to tell me that she had some news she wanted to share and could I phone her when I had some free time. FREE TIME! What is free time? Anyway, knowing Mum, I knew it would be important.

Mum warned me that what she was going to tell me may upset me but she stated that she would rather I heard the news from her than from anyone else. Annabelle had contacted her by phone, as she again desperately needed to talk to someone who she could trust. Mum wasn't keen on seeing her, but felt that Annabelle really needed a friend, so she decided to invite her around for a coffee last evening after dinner.

Obviously, when Annabelle arrived all she wanted to do was to talk about Cassandra. Mum related the recent developments to me and told me that Cassandra had REALLY overstepped the mark this time. The dramatic events had happened when she had visited her father for the weekend. She had been showing signs of being insanely jealous of her step mother's daughters who are much younger than her. Dominic and his new wife Sophie had noticed her recent behaviour. It was obvious to them that Cassandra had been feeling unable to cope with the attention that her father had been paying the girls. Even though he had been making an extra effort to make Cassandra feel part of the new family, the tension had remained.

WELL, Sophie had walked into the family bathroom, and had been horrified to find her daughters being held hostage in the corner of the shower recess by Cassandra. The latter was threatening the young girls with a pair of pointed scissors which she was holding in the direction of the eldest daughter's throat.

It really is too terrible to imagine. Without going into all of the details, it would appear that she had been threatening them in this way on a regular basis over the last few weeks. Her idea was to pressurize the girls into stealing their mother's jewellery. She had gone as far as to tell them that if they failed to carry out her requests they would be stabbed.

Sophie immediately called for Dominic, who on realising the severity of the problem, had immediately phoned for the family doctor.

I knew then that I had to call a halt to the phone call. I didn't want to hear anymore. I was horrified; such strong memories swiftly came flooding back filling me with anguish. Emotions that I thought I had dealt with, dusted and put away forever returned in an instant. Strong hot waves of panic engulfed me, I became hot and clammy, my heart was pounding in my chest and I found breathing difficult.

I couldn't concentrate on anything at that moment. Immediately, I knew I must see if Gillie was free. I knew that I could talk to her in confidence. I desperately needed to talk about this. I felt really shaken up, a total wreck!

Two hours later.

Thankfully Gillie made herself free for me as she could immediately tell I needed her. It's the first time I've experienced a panic attack. Gillie sat with me, helped me to take control of my breathing, and just listened.

My first reaction after I'd calmed down, was to feel embarrassed. I really thought I had over reacted. Gillie explained that it was a deep seated reaction to the trauma of the bullying I had encountered at St Ursula's. She asked me if I had had any counselling. When I replied that I hadn't, she described my outburst to Cassandra's behaviour as perhaps being a positive thing that had happened and that I should not feel ashamed. She explained that it was a healthy way of getting it out of the system and that I was not to feel uncomfortable. However, she did say that if I had any more attacks similar to this one, it may be an idea to speak to a professional counsellor about it. She assured me that no one would know about this episode apart from her.

However, she suggested that I phone Mum to let her know I was OK. I had cut the call so abruptly as I had been so panic-stricken. I hadn't given a thought as to what Mum was thinking.

Later that evening, I felt calm enough to call Mum. I'm so appreciative that I now have people I can talk to. It's so important.

Still finding it difficult to understand what makes people behave like this.

Amanda

Term 2 Entry 18

Dear H,

Awesome! Tonight's a special night! We have a barbeque/ disco arranged for this evening. Everyone is looking forward to a social and there's a real buzz about the place today. It will do everyone good. With not long now until the concert, things are hotting up, in fact they are 'sizzling'! We all need to take time out before the concert gives us all a nervous breakdown... only kidding!

Simon has been busy with his classical guitar studies in preparation for his solo performance at the concert. He whispered to Immie and me that RELIEF are planning a surprise appearance at the barbeque tonight. He says it will be good for the band members to play again in public, as for the first time, they've been invited to perform at the concert and they need to play in front of a live audience. I can't wait.

I don't think I told you that the Academy usually arranges a movie night or something similar for most Saturday evenings. We also have options to go in small arranged groups to concerts and performances in the city but they only happen if there is something really worth attending. Occasionally, we have visiting professional musicians who perform for us. These are quite grand occasions. The last one featured a fabulous group of three young violinists who have recently graduated from Uni. They played classics with a modern twist and they wore really trendy black leather.

However, I think this evening will be cool, a barbeque AND RELIEF!!!

Not long now. Big decision time... what to wear! I'll ask Immie what she's thinking of wearing. I hope she's already decided. I really don't think I can cope with six changes of clothes this evening! It's time to go and check.

Clothes strewn on the bed,
Scattered all over the floor,
Tangled on their hangers,
Clothes lying in a mess everywhere!
I've tried on everything I've got
And I have NOTHING TO WEAR!!

Girls must be girls!

Amanda

Term 2 Entry 19

Dear H,

I've just received a very long email containing numerous attachments and useful websites from Emma. She has been busy! She must have been glued to her iPad! She has found out a lot of information about setting up a Daisy Chain group. It's not as easy as I first thought. Lots of things to think about. I will definitely need the help of Gillie.

Emma also suggested I share this information with Gillie and that, during the next school holiday, I can meet up with her for a long chat about all of this. That's sounds great! I'm really looking forward to it. Although we need to get a Daisy Chain organised as soon as possible, it's something that needs to be done properly. At present, everyone is rushed off their feet, so the beginning of next term would be an excellent time to get it off the ground and running.

I'll see if Gillie is available and ask if it's OK to forward the information on to her.

Feeling positive.

Amanda

Term 2 Entry 20

Dear H,

Last night we had the dress rehearsal for the concert which will be held this evening. It didn't go too badly, but it could have been better. Everyone's nerves seemed to be on edge and some people revealed a different side of their personalities to the ones we normally see. There were scowls, tears, bursts of temper and one person stamped their feet and stormed off the stage in frustration. (Not good!) By the end of the rehearsal, the major problems appeared to have been sorted out, so fingers AND toes crossed for this evening. Thankfully, everyone has the chance for a final run through of their individual items with their tutors this afternoon so, any niggles can be sorted out.

Mum, Dad and Gran have texted to tell me they have arrived at the nearby hotel where they'll stay for tonight and then I'll travel back home with Mum and Dad tomorrow for the two week break.

From a 'slightly nervy'

Amanda

Winter Holiday, Entry 1

Dear H,

Well, I'm now home for two weeks. I just didn't realise how much nervous energy I was burning during the build-up to the concert. Now that I'm home, I feel absolutely shattered. The first morning, I didn't wake up until nearly lunch time and I still felt exhausted. Thankfully, Mum just left me to sleep.

Firstly, I must tell you about the concert. It was absolutely FABULOUS! After everyone had completed their final run throughs with their tutors, and returned to Grantham House, there was a hub of nervous excitement and activity. Some of the girls raced off to the village for hair appointments etc. It appeared that anyone or, in fact, anybody who was offering services such as make-up and nails had been fully booked for weeks. As the village is small and there is only the one hairdressing salon, the college had set aside a room and invited some of the staff from one of the hairdressing salons in the nearby town to offer their services. They had turned up in a mini bus crammed full of bags and cases brimming with hair equipment and dryers.

Mum had offered to call round before the concert and help Immie and me get ready. She's really good with makeup and nail polish. She had not met Immie before, but they hit it off immediately. Immie's parents were flying in from Singapore but wouldn't be arriving until just before the concert.

Wearing THE DRESS was something I had been dying to do for weeks. It had been hanging in my wardrobe in a black dress bag for protection. Every so often, I had unzipped the bag cover and gazed in admiration at the dress. It gave me goose bumps just looking at it. By the time I was ready to wear it, and Mum had decided where to place the silk flower for the best effect, I was shivering with excitement. It made me feel like a different person, so grown up. It was magical. I don't think I will ever forget hearing the swish of the skirt and feeling the layers of the taffeta underskirt brush against my legs as I walked across to the concert hall. I looked at Immie, who also looked terrific, and said to her with a big grin on my face, "We really scrub up well don't you think!"

Thankfully, everything went off really smoothly. By the time the orchestra members were positioned on the stage in readiness to begin, everyone appeared to be in control of their nerves. The only one who seemed to 'loose it' and not be in control was Jessica. She was behind stage and appeared to be a nervous wreck. With shoulders hunched, she was pacing backwards and forwards in a very agitated manner and muttering repeatedly, "I can't do it. I can't do it."

Thankfully, one of the tutors realised what was happening and led her gently away to a quiet side room before any of us, who were waiting to perform, began to pick up on her anxiety. She wasn't due to perform until the second half of the concert, so had some time in which to calm down. She reappeared just before she was due to perform and seemed to be calmer and more in charge of herself. She managed to play well but she appeared to be very low in spirits. I was really surprised and wondered if she was always like that prior to performing. Perhaps that is why she was so mean to Immie. Immie always gives off this aura of being in full control - even if she isn't. Jessica either seems to be full-on and I mean 'FULL-ON' or depressed. I can't work her out.

My solos went well, but the best thing for me that evening was when 'The Daisy Chain' was announced. It was a surprise item chosen to conclude the first half of the concert. I felt so proud when Simon, Immie and I stood together on the stage. I listened to the opening bars of the music and lost myself in the meaning of the words which meant SO MUCH to me. As the applause quietened down and we left the stage, I burst into tears, tears of joy, relief and an overwhelming sense of pride.

Mum, Dad and Gran were ecstatic. The song had come as a complete surprise to them. After the concert, Mum took lots of photos of the three of us. She couldn't stop telling me how proud she was and Dad, not generally known for his shows of affection, grasped me in a big bear hug. That, for me, was the icing on the cake.

It was really hard to sleep that night. The adrenalin was pumping through my veins. Everyone stayed up really late, played music and talked until Gillie arrived to tell us that if we weren't tired, she was and it was time for us all to go to bed.

The morning after the concert, Mum, Dad and Gran arranged for us all to meet up with Simon and Immie's parents at the hotel for a scrumptious Morning Tea before we all said our 'Good byes' and flew off in different directions. I noticed Mum was having an animated chat with Immie's parents. I don't know what on earth she was talking about but it appeared very in-depth, if you know what I mean. Afterwards, when questioned, she didn't appear to understand what I was talking about! I don't believe her. She's hiding something!

Still feeling on a high,

Amanda

Winter Holiday, Entry 2

Dear H,

I've just returned from meeting Emma. I was totally
surprised. She had texted me the previous evening saying,
"Meet you tomorrow at 10 in the coffee shop." There was
nothing unusual about that. When I arrived, there she was on
her own sitting proudly in a brand new bright purple battery
operated wheelchair.

"What do you think to this?" she asked me with a great big
grin stretching from ear to ear.

To tell the truth, I was quite stunned. It's the first time I've
seen Emma out by herself. This new wheelchair is just great
for Emma.

"I feel free for the first time since the accident!" she
exclaimed with delight as she twirled around in a circle.
Thankfully, the coffee shop has an empty space in the centre
so she didn't have any accidents with flying coffee cups! The
owners also showed their pleasure by joining in with a round
of applause and shouted us to complimentary hot chocolates.

Emma had previously shared with me how frustrated she
had felt having to be taken everywhere by her mum, so this
latest chair has made such a difference to her. I could see it

myself. She seemed more vibrant and confident. Just imagine being sixteen and never being allowed to go anywhere on your own.

Last term she had gone out of her way to research as much information for me about the setting up of a Daisy Chain. The positive thing I really like is that although there are Daisy Chains already operating, the rules aren't quite the same. This means that you can set up a Daisy Chain according to the needs of a particular group of people. I'd ploughed through the different information about the already existing groups but wanted to relive my own experiences so I could explain what I thought was important. I thought it would be a good idea to write down as much as I could so, when I discussed it later with Gillie, we had a starting point.

Emma helped me to make up the following list. At this stage, it's very basic. We both felt that everyone's experiences of bullying are different and that how they react to the bullying is also individual. There are no hard and fast rules as the situation dictates how a Daisy Chain group is run, so here goes,

DAISY CHAIN

- Daisy Chain is the anti-bullying emblem
- All members genuinely need to have experienced bullying or are presently being bullied
- Strategies need to be discussed as to how best to respond to bullies
- Members need to feel supported and safe at all times
- Meetings need to be arranged on a regular basis as required by that group
- Members need to be able to discuss their problems in confidence
- Ideally, each member should have a 'personal mentor'
- Access at all times, by phone, email etc, to mentoring , peer support, older students, adult volunteers etc
- Members should have the chance to be able to speak individually to a counsellor if they are not comfortable discussing their problems in a group situation
- There should be access to professional help if required, i.e. a qualified psychologist, medical assistance etc
- Strategies for dealing with bullying, e.g. talks on self-esteem, depression, weight loss etc to be arranged
- Informal 'fun' evenings to be arranged

Well, that's a start. What do you think? Can you think of anything else I can include? I think, for me, the worst thing was feeling so isolated and helpless. That was the hardest thing to cope with, apart from the bullying itself of course. Then there was the depression, followed by binge eating and the obvious gain in weight. Then I really was on a downward spiral. I don't know how I managed to survive through all of it especially when I think of all of the terrible emails, texts and verbal comments that were flung in my direction. Reading up about bullying on social media, I think I came off lightly compared to some people. There are some dreadful articles which I don't want to share with you as I find them too upsetting. I'm sure you'll have an idea of what I'm talking about.

It wasn't until I had Gran to confide in and the introduction to my new interest in singing that I began my journey of recovery. Although I now feel a different person, an experience such as listening to the story of Cassandra's exploits, can easily take me back to that terrible time. I think that is what is referred to as Post-Traumatic Stress Disorder (PTSD for short).

Life's complicated,
Amanda

Winter Holiday, Entry 3

Dear H,

I just had to share this latest news with you. Mum has just returned from the gym. Annabelle was there apparently peddling frantically on the exercise bike as if she was being chased by a charging bull. She had a fierce determination written across her face. Mum said she looked awful. Her long blonde hair was scraped back in a pony tail and was showing a lot of re-growth. Her face was bare of make-up and she appeared pale and drawn, definitely not her usual immaculate self. She caught up with Mum in the changing room. She explained that she was a nervous wreck trying to cope with the trauma associated with Cassandra.

She told mum that after the 'scissor' incident in the bathroom, Dominic had immediately called the family doctor to the scene. When he heard what had happened, and witnessed how traumatised the young girls were, he insisted that Cassandra be removed from the house, well away from the girls and that she underwent professional therapy.

Cassandra has now been banished to stay with an aunt, Dominic's older sister, Rose, and has been enrolled at another school on the other side of the city. She's undergoing intensive therapy with a specialist psychologist. It was thought a fresh start in a new environment would be good for her.

However, Cassandra is finding the new situation difficult, especially as Aunt Rose has set strict rules which Cassandra is finding hard to accept. Consequently, she has been phoning her mother every night pleading with her to let her come home. Annabelle says it is wearing her down. The constant crying and promises to be good are beginning to make Annabelle feel guilty. Why Annabelle should feel guilty, I'm not sure, but Cassandra is very good at manipulating people and working on their weaknesses.

Annabelle continued with the story and admitted that she had very nearly given in and let Cassandra return home. She knows deep down that Cassandra requires help and that Dominic would be fuming with her if she gave in to her daughter's demands. She said that although she and Dominic are divorced, she wants to remain friends with him, and for both of them to be available to offer support to their daughter. They have agreed to review the situation after a six month trial period. Presently, both parents visit her but she's not allowed to have any contact with her two step-sisters.

The young traumatised sisters are also undergoing counselling. Dominic thought it was necessary as both of them had been having nightmares and were terrified of going into the bathroom on their own even though Cassandra was no longer in the house. Dominic was scared that the frightening experience could lead to them suffering from PTSD.

Well, only a few more days and it's back to the Academy. I still don't know what Mum has planned, if anything, for my birthday. She's leaving it a bit late. I know she's been making phone calls but refuses to tell me who she's been talking to.

Anyway, a shopping trip and a visit to Philippe are planned for tomorrow... can't wait.

Never a dull moment!

Amanda

PS I nearly forgot to tell you that I had spent an afternoon with Mrs Field. She told me that as I was no longer a student of hers, I could call her Holly. She was really keen to hear about the concert, my dress AND the song, 'The Daisy Chain'. Of course, she wanted to hear me sing it. Simon had kindly given me a backing CD which he had recorded with Immie. I think she was impressed. She didn't say a lot, she never does. However, I noticed her wiping away a few tears which I don't think she wanted me to see.

Term 3 Entry 1

Dear H,

Well, Immie and I have safely returned to the Academy for Term Three. We are now halfway through the year. How time flies!

Before I go any further, I must tell you about my birthday celebrations. NO, not the celebrations I shared with Gran on the actual day but the one Mum had promised me. I couldn't fit in a writing session before I left home as it was SO full on, so here goes!

I was due to return to the Academy on the Monday as term officially began on the Tuesday. It was now the last Saturday of the holiday break and, as I had mentioned to you, still nothing had happened about my birthday. Mum had been behaving strangely whenever I mentioned my birthday. She didn't answer my questions and immediately changed the topic of conversation which wasn't like her at all. I knew she hadn't forgotten but by now, I was beginning to think that NOTHING was going to happen, no celebrations, NOTHING!! I know I had mentioned that I wasn't a party girl and I didn't like surprises BUT I would have liked something to have happened! Mum was up early on the Saturday morning. She called out before she left, "Amanda, you need to be up and dressed before I return."

"What's so important?" I queried.

"Make sure you wear one of your new outfits," she said as she made a quick departure.

I began to feel a tiny bit excited, a slight fluttering in the tummy. Was this something to do with my birthday I wondered? I decided that it MUST be something to do with it. I just hoped Mum hadn't gone to extremes and planned a celebration with themes!

The time passed slowly. I had eventually decided on wearing one of my new dresses and had matched it with a pair of leggings and flat pumps. Then, I thought, no, I'd look better in a new pair of jeans and a top. Then I wondered if we were going out, so changed back into the dress and leggings again. I'm almost as bad as Immie with her frequent changes of clothes! I waited and waited. I had looked out of the window SO many times. Dad was in the office in the city for the morning and I didn't want to bother him. I decided to ring Gran, but there was no answer. Strange I thought.

Eventually, I heard the car door bang, not once but three times. I raced to the window and I couldn't believe my eyes. There standing in the driveway clutching a suitcase was IMMIE! Then she was joined by Gran holding a much smaller case! I was so surprised. I raced down the stairs at record breaking speed just as Immie was entering the hall. I flung my arms around her.

"What are you doing here?" I asked excitedly, "and Gran as well!" I exclaimed.

"Well, isn't it time we celebrated your birthday? It's way over time," Mum said with an innocent expression on her face.

I couldn't believe it. Mum had arranged this with Immie's parents during the Morning Tea on the last day of last term. She had asked if Immie could return from Singapore early, fly directly to us, stay a couple of nights and then we could return to the Academy by plane together.

I was ecstatic. I forgave Mum for this surprise. After Immie and Gran had recovered from their flights, not that Immie really needed to recover, she was as excited as I was, Dad arrived home from the office and we all went out for lunch. Just before we left I'd asked if Emma could come too. Mum replied, "All taken care of."

Mum had secretly arranged a light lunch at a bistro near to Emma's house. She had made sure that it could accommodate Emma's new wheelchair. It was the first time that Emma had met Immie, but we all got on tremendously well. The adults couldn't get a word in. Later, Mum said how great it was to see me so happy.

Mum explained that as Immie and I had to return to the
Academy early on the Monday morning, that it would be better
to have the major celebration on the Saturday evening. After
lunch we returned home, after making sure that Emma was fine
to travel home independently. Mum suggested that we all have
a relaxing afternoon but that first, I was to open my gifts.
Mum and Dad presented me with a wonderful watch, one that
I can keep for special occasions such as when I'm performing.
She also gave me a few bits and bobs, CDs, perfume and makeup.
Gran gave me a silver linked heart bracelet and a brand new
journal. She said, "I know how you like writing. You must have
filled up the one I bought for you last year. I hope you don't
think it's boring."

Brilliant! Little does she know how much I write and how useful
it will be.

Immie gave me a heart shaped jewellery box which swivels open,
which I'm going to find useful. I will treasure it always.

I then opened my cards and was surprised to find a funny one
from Simon. Inside, he'd written, "Please don't burst into tears!
Have a happy day."

Cheekily, he had folded a single tissue and placed it inside the card.
Wait until I see him next week!

Gran wanted to have a rest so I showed Immie around the house and then we locked ourselves away in my room and had a long 'girl talk' and played some music.

Later that afternoon, Mum suggested I change into one of my more formal dresses and Immie disappeared to change as well. When everyone was ready, we set off. Mum had mentioned a surprise so I didn't ask any questions. Off we headed towards the city. My tummy was all abuzz with excitement. We arrived at one of the top restaurants and after a superb dinner, we headed off to the theatre to see 'The Lion King'. I was enchanted by the colourful costumes and the vibrancy of the performance in general. It was a wonderful evening and we all staggered home full of gorgeous food and with music swirling around in our heads.

Sunday, was pretty low key. Immie and I wandered round to the local coffee shop to meet up with Emma and the Purple People Eater, as she has decided to call her new wheelchair. After we'd ordered, Emma gave me her present. I was really thrilled as it was a pair of glittery silver earrings with a blue stone. "You can wear them on stage. I bought them to match your dress," she said thoughtfully.

Well, after the catch-up with Emma, we returned home. I had some last minute packing to do and I wanted to spend some time with Gran.

It really was a great birthday. Thankfully, Mum understands
me better than she used to. She knows that her idea of a big
birthday bash, lots of noise and lots of people isn't my scene.
We've come a long way, my Mum and me.

Love you Mum,

Amanda

Term 3 Entry 2

Dear H,

The second piece of news I have to share with you this term isn't so cheerful and concerns Tilly. Immie and I had only just arrived back when we were hit with the hot topic of conversation. Tilly has apparently left the Academy as she's pregnant. The senior girls, who used to be Tilly's friends, are all gossiping in groups. They are saying they knew all about the pregnancy all the time, as if! You should hear the horrible things they are saying about her. I was hoping the 'Tilly' rumours whispered last term weren't true. There's a new girl in her room. I haven't had a chance to speak to her yet.

Perhaps I shouldn't, but I feel sorry for Tilly. I wasn't aware until recently that her mother had died a year ago. When I told Gran about it, she suggested that Tilly may have become involved with Jacques because she needed someone to make her feel special. I hadn't given it much thought but Gran always appears to be able to see both sides of a story.

It has now been confirmed that Tilly has had to leave the Academy. Amy, who used to be her best friend, made the announcement to everyone that it had been 'kindly' suggested to Tilly, that due to the intensive academic and music program, that no way could she continue with her studies if she had a baby to look after. It's true, it takes us all of our time to fit everything in and we only have ourselves to look after.

It appears she received this news over the phone whilst she was at home during the holiday and was heartbroken. The Academy first spoke to her father who had no idea of the situation. He, according to Amy, was so angry and disappointed with her that he said he doesn't want to see her for a while. Imagine that! I can't begin to imagine how she must be feeling, first of all having to admit to the pregnancy and then to be told to leave the house. Thankfully, Jacques' parents have shown empathy and offered her a home with them for the immediate future. The Academy says she can still continue to study the flute privately with her tutor. However, it won't be the same for her ever again.

Lots to think about,

Amanda

Term 3 Entry 3

Dear H,

Well, we really know our Winter holiday is over! We've been hit with SO MUCH WORK! Thankfully, we don't have a concert to prepare for at the end of this term.

Immie and I have both opted to do Dance as our Sports Option for this term. It should be fun.

I've just said, "Hi," to the new girl, the one who has replaced Tilly. She introduced herself to me. Her name is Charlotte. As soon as she spoke, I couldn't help but notice her stammer. She told me that she has been having therapy for it and, as long as she takes her time speaking, she is able to control the stammer. It only gets worse if she's under pressure. Luckily her music specialisation is Modern Dance so it shouldn't be a problem as she won't be required to speak on stage. She added that she had been on a waiting list to attend the Academy and as Tilly had left, she had been offered a place. "Immie and I are just up the corridor if you need anything," I added.

I hadn't been in my room more than ten minutes when I heard a voice I instantly recognised, "Ch...Ch...Ch...Charlotte, Ch...Ch...Ch...Charlotte," followed by loud maniacal laughter.

By the time, I had reached the door, the offending Jessica

had disappeared. I raced up the corridor to Charlotte's room. "Are you OK?"

"Y...yes, I'm. f...fine. I'm used to it," she replied.

"Jessica is a pain and it's NOT fine," I replied.

I was SO angry. I rushed off to find Gillie. "We've GOT to get a Daisy Chain started," I blurted.

"Yes, I know but what's brought this on today?" asked Gillie.

"Jessica is imitating the new girl with the stammer," I announced.

Gillie responded, "Oh, I see. I'm not surprised. Leave it with me. I'll arrange a meeting ASAP."

I replied with relief, "Thanks, I knew you'd understand."

I went straight off to inform Immie. "Would you mind if I attended the meeting?" she asked.

"Of course you can," I replied. I knew I could rely on her. That's what friends are for.

From a 'somewhat annoyed', Amanda

Term 3 Entry 4

Dear H,

Strange news is dominating the scene! I don't know what has happened but since Jessica was heard imitating Charlotte, she suddenly appears to have lost the plot. I didn't notice it at first as I've been so occupied with the Daisy Chain. However, the girl who has always been so noisy and irritating is now walking around in a daze and appears depressed. She looks as if she's not 'with-it'. Her hair is a total mess, uncombed and lank and her clothes are crumpled.

This is the first I've heard of it but rumour has it, although you can't believe everything you hear, is that her tutors have not been happy with her grades recently and she hasn't practised the piano for two weeks. Continuing with the rumours, again no proof, her work has really hit rock bottom and she's been given a warning, that if she doesn't improve she will lose her place at the Academy. The girls at her end of the corridor are saying they don't think she's been going to bed at night. Some of them with rooms close to her have been complaining about her disturbing them and keeping them awake. Again, I don't know if that is true.

Although she's not my favourite person, I feel concerned. Something is definitely not right.
Feeling worried, Amanda

Term 3 Entry 5

Dear H,

Brilliant! So excited and apprehensive at the same time! We have set a time and a date for our initial meeting of the Daisy Chain. This meeting is really to have an informal chat about what we think the Daisy Chain should be all about. I've had another chat with Emma and Gran and mentioned it briefly to Mum. One thing Gran questioned was how we could fund any visits to professionals, such as counsellors, if they were required. I had become so carried away with the idea but hadn't thought of having to pay for professional services. Hopefully, Gillie may have given it some thought and will come up with some bright ideas on this.

At the present time, the meeting only consists of Gillie, Immie and me. However, I did think of inviting Simon but, as Immie reminded me, the name Daisy Chain would only appeal to girls. Perhaps, when we've got the Daisy Chain up and running, we could think of a suitable name for a group aimed at males. I think we have enough to do establishing a girls' group at the moment, but it's certainly something to bear in mind for the future.

Just a thought! Perhaps a good name for a boys' group might be the Bike Chain. I may suggest it to Simon and see what he thinks, on the other hand, perhaps not at the moment. Sorry, my mind is spiralling in all directions. Concentrate Amanda! I have enough to do with the Daisy Chain for the time being.

I have to go to rehearse now for a charity concert at which I've been invited to perform. This came out of the blue. It's quite an honour and I'm so excited. Luckily, Immie is playing the piano accompaniment for me.

These concerts crop up from time to time but it's the first time I've been asked to perform. It's usually the more senior students who are invited.

There are so many charities that require money. This one is being held for breast cancer research. I did hear that Tilly had lost her mum to breast cancer and it made singing at the concert more of a personal thing, even though I had never met her mother. However, I did see how her death had had such a devastating impact on Tilly. The repercussions are enormous. It must be terrible to lose your mother when you are so young. Well, terrible to lose your mother at any age. I wondered how I would feel if I lost a family member to cancer. I know how I 'think' I would feel but, I suppose, unless it happens to you, you would really have no idea.

I'm a very fortunate person. To be able to share my gift of singing to assist people who are less fortunate than me is quite overwhelming. I hope this last sentence doesn't make me sound like a prig. It's not meant in that way at all. I just feel that if I can help someone by using my voice, then I should.

Anyway, I think I had better go. I can hear Immie locking her door, so she'll be banging on my door in a second.

Bye for now,
Amanda

Term 3 Entry 6

Dear H,

Wow! The charity concert was a huge success. It was held in a large hall in the nearby town. A few other students had been invited to perform as well as myself and Immie, so we were taken there and back in the school mini bus. Mr Taylor, one of the music teachers, drove the bus and Gillie kindly went along as she had a night off from her Housemother duties. We weren't the only performers there, but we were made to feel so special. The ticket sales and donations raised a substantial amount of money and the organisers were thrilled. I would like to be involved in more concerts like this. It's such an easy thing for me to do. It would be very wrong of me to refuse.

I must return to my homework. Gillie has put aside some time later this evening to spend with Immie and me to discuss the setting up of a Daisy Chain group. Thankfully, we do not have a concert at the end of this term, so there's time to slot in a few other things. If someone had told me that this year I'd be involved in so many things AND have the confidence to carry them out, I would have told them they were stupid and that they didn't know what they were talking about. I just couldn't have imagined doing all of these things when I first came to the Academy. Now, I've got into a routine, and as long as I keep to deadlines, everything is fine.
Back to work, Amanda

Term 3 Entry 7

Dear H,

Just what I need! I've got so much going on at the moment that the last thing I wanted was to see Signora De Luca heading purposely in my direction as I walked along the path to the block. Her plump arms were waving in the air and multiple glittering bracelets were clinking. She was a complete vision of purple chiffon on the move. Can you imagine! I'm sure she'd even had a violet tint run through her hair since the last time I saw her. Signora De Luca is quite short and plump and makes her presence felt by a very loud penetrating voice.

"Amarndaaaaa!" she screamed. Everyone in the surrounding area stopped what they were doing and turned to stare at ME. She continued at the top of her voice, "You are the girl with the gift, the gift of THE most marvellous voice. I see you on stage at La Scala in Milan, adored by your fans."

I was so embarrassed; I just stopped in my tracks. I felt rooted to the spot, virtually couldn't move and waited apprehensively for her to approach me.

She arrived, completely out of breath, still talking at the same pitch. In between gulps of air she continued, "Amarnda, you need to learn Italian. It is absolutely essential for your operatic training. I will speak to your parents so that we can organise this. Lessons will begin next year."

With that ultimatum, she stormed off presumably to 'attack' another student. Out of the corner of my eye, half hiding behind a bush, I could see Immie doubled up, clutching her stomach with one hand and trying to hold back her giggles with the other. She had watched the whole scene without me knowing.

I turned to see her and said, "It's NOT funny! For a start, I have NO plans to be an opera singer! What am I going to do?"

Immie replied patiently, once she'd controlled her giggles and could see I was quite upset, "Don't worry. She can't just go ahead without consulting other teachers."

When she saw by my expression that I was really concerned, she asked me, "Are the lessons beginning this week?"

"No," I replied tentatively.

"Are they going to begin this term?"

"No," I answered more firmly.

"Are they going to begin this school year?"

"No," I replied with conviction.

Immie said, "Well, stop worrying. It's a waste of time worrying about something that may never happen."

I replied, "Yes, I suppose you are right."

"Anyway," she continued with a cheeky grin on her face, "you never know, you may change your mind. I can just see you on stage warbling away at the top of your voice!"

By now, she'd brought a smile to my face. What Immie said was true, it's not worth worrying about something that may never happen.

"Come on," Immie urged, "we've got to work on the Daisy Chain. That's more important than anything else at the moment."

Worry is a waste of time!

From 'Amarnda'

PS Even so, I still think I'll warn Mum and Dad that they may receive a call from Signora De Luca and tell them that they are to ignore her! Opera singer, I DON'T THINK!

Term 3 Entry 8

Dear H,

The first informal meeting of the Daisy Chain went off really well, even better than I had expected. We each had copies of the list I had previously made. We agreed with all of the items, especially that anyone being bullied needs support and 'someone' to share the burden. We also discussed that each Daisy Chain could be adapted to the situation as not all groups may need to include all of the items on our agenda. We all felt that the Daisy Chain needed to meet on a regular basis and that in the beginning, members would be invited individually to attend or be sponsored by someone who knew of their situation.

We then began to talk about the more serious issues of any members who needed more professional assistance. Gillie suggested we have a list of people who we could invite to attend meetings, give talks on special subjects etc. These could have a medical, teaching, counselling background or something similar. Gillie suggested that it wasn't necessary for these people to attend every meeting. She said she knew a few of the local people who may be interested. Some of them may wish to become mentors to students who needed one-on-one help, someone who would be there for them either in person or via email or phone.

"What about students who need specialised help?" I asked.

Gillie replied, "Well, I've been giving that a lot of thought and I've come up with an idea."

Immie and I sat on the edge of our seats and held our breath. Gillie went on to explain. "How about organising a disco twice a year with extra entertainment organised by the college? I'm sure if you two twisted Simon and the rest of the RELIEF members around your little fingers, you could persuade them to perform. It could be a ticketed event in the village hall, nothing like our concerts here, far less formal. There could be supporting acts and I'm sure you and Immie could perform a few songs.

I also have another idea and that is that you, Immie and Simon go into the recording studio and record the 'The Daisy Chain' song. It could be released as a single and sold for a small amount. There would be no fees for the use of the studio. The profit could be donated to the Daisy Chain for private medical appointments."

Immie and I looked at each other. We didn't know whether to laugh or cry. We were so overcome with emotion.

"Wow, that would be absolutely fabulous! Thank you SO MUCH," we both said in unison.

Gillie replied, "I can ask for some other members of staff to help organise the event. I know you have your music and Academy work to concentrate on. I think it'll be fun. Leave it with me."

I couldn't believe it. As we left Gillie's flat we joyfully danced down the corridor.

Lots to think about,

Amanda

Term 3 Entry 9

Dear H,

Well, it's all go, go, go! Immie and I are SO excited about the proposed Daisy Chain disco. It's all we can think and talk about at the moment. Of course, we had to share the news with the most important people in our lives, my parents who were thrilled, Gran and Emma who were both ecstatic. Immie's parents were also very proud.

We managed to catch Simon as he was leaving the Block after his private guitar lesson. "Gillie has told us we have to twist you and the other members of RELIEF around our little fingers," we blurted out before exploding into giggles.

Simon, appearing suspicious asked, "WHAT'S it all about? Come on, stop this hysterical giggling."

We managed to explain about the meeting with Gillie, all about the Daisy Chain and the disco/concert to raise money. We kept the best bit until last. "...and WE ARE GOING TO RECORD 'THE DAISY CHAIN!'" we exclaimed together.

"WOW, that's really awesome!" he replied enthusiastically.

After we'd calmed down, we asked Simon if he thought RELIEF would be willing to gig at the disco. He told us he thought there wouldn't be any problems but to leave it with him.

Now, all we have to do is leave it to Gillie to inform us of her plans, rehearse for the recording, and prepare our items for performing at the disco, and keep up with our school work etc, try to fit in our Sport option and my cycling. Not much to ask is it?

No time to get bored.

Amanda

Term 3 Entry 10

Dear H,

SO EXCITED! It's a dream come true. Remember when I first stepped inside the Recording Studio and I said it would make my day if I was ever allowed to record a song there? Well, IT'S ACTUALLY HAPPENED! Gillie has been working away frantically to organise the fund raising disco in the village hall AND, we three, Simon, Immie and I have recorded 'The Daisy Chain'. HOW AMAZING IS THAT!

One of the senior students, Dave, who has been studying to be a sound engineer, offered his services to us for free. Gillie told us he was an expert and had already been snapped up and offered a position to work at one of the recording studios with a leading label when he leaves here at the end of the year.

It really was a thrilling experience. Dave sat in a room with a huge console covered with numbers, dials and knobs. From his seat in front of the console, he had a superb view of the studio through a large window. The studio contained a grand piano and lots of microphones, some suspended from the ceiling and others on stands. This was where we were to perform.

Dave told us to relax and to make ourselves feel at home. Immie sat at the piano. He asked us to perform a few bars of the song while he adjusted the microphones. I sang the

song a few times with Immie and Simon accompanying me.
I wanted to make sure my voice felt warmed up. Gillie then
appeared in the room with Dave and gave us a wave.

The fourth time we performed the song, Dave said, "Great!
Wonderful! Awesome!"

"Are we going to record it this time?" Simon asked.

We were so taken aback when Dave replied, "We've just done
it. With some professional recordings, the vocalist will record
a line at a time, but you guys were so fantastic, you hit it on
the head, first time round. I don't think we can improve upon
it. What do you think Gillie?"

"I've heard you perform that song so many times before and
that was the best I've ever heard it. Congratulations, I feel
very proud of you. Would you like to hear the recording?"

"Yes please," we chorused in unison.

Dave played the recording to us and we all sat in silence. I had
never heard a recording of myself singing before. I was SO
taken aback. "Is that really me?"

"Of course it's you," replied Simon. "Who else do you think it is?"

I was so overwhelmed and speechless. Gillie asked, "What do you think to it Amanda?'

As a reply, I burst into tears. Simon said, "Oh no, here she goes again. I knew we should have bought the tissues."

I knew he was trying his best to lighten the moment. My tears were tears of pure joy. The recording was everything I'd ever imagined it to be, but better, if that makes sense.

After the awkward moment had passed and Simon has assured Dave, that I really was happy with the result, we all hugged each other. I don't think I've ever felt so happy before, not even when I won the scholarship to St C's AND I was certainly happy then. This time it wasn't just being happy. I felt ecstatic as if all my birthdays and Christmases had been rolled into one.

> I'm bubbling!
> I'm bursting!
> I'm floating!
> I'm flying!
> I'm spinning and soaring!
> OH
> WHAT A FEELING!

Life couldn't get any better!
Amanda

Term 3 Entry 11

Dear H,

I've been on such a high ever since we recorded 'The Daisy Chain'. It has really lifted my spirits and I've felt just great. Gillie has organised the single CD in readiness for the disco. I've already sent copies to my parents, Gran and Emma. Now, Gillie is busy advertising the disco. We need to get as many people there as possible. She's even contacted the local radio station and the local paper. It's SO exciting! Who would have thought that all of this had evolved through me being bullied? Of course, Emma played a huge part for introducing me to the Daisy Chain. I can never say it enough, Emma IS THE MOST AMAZING FRIEND!

From a very thankful,
Amanda

Term 3 Entry 12

Dear H,

Immie and I have just returned from a trip to the village. Gillie had asked us to distribute some posters advertising the disco. When we were in the Post Office delivering the last poster to be displayed in the Post Office window, we bumped into Tilly. We both said, "Hi, How are you?"

She returned our greeting with a watery smile. She certainly didn't look very happy and turned her eyes to look down on her growing bump with embarrassment. Her complexion appeared dull and pale, definitely no glow there, in fact, she gave the appearance of looking shattered, as though she needed a few good nights of sleep. On the spur of the moment, Immie said, "We're going to the Coffee Shop before we return to the Academy. Have you time to join us?"

Poor Tilly looked as if we had offered her a win on the Lotto. Without a thought, she replied instantly with, "I'd love to. It's so kind of you to ask."

We both were given the impression that things weren't very good for her. We settled at a corner table, out of the way and waited for our order. Tilly told us that as she had had to leave the Academy she was finishing her last year of school by Distance Education. This means, she was submitting all of her assignments by post. That had been her reason to visit the Post Office. With tears in her eyes, she told us how much she was missing the Academy and having contact with the girls. It appears a lot of her friends, even Amy, who had been her best friend, had now chosen to ignore her since she had become pregnant. Even when she had visited the Academy once a week for her flute lesson, she had been snubbed.

It was like opening 'the flood gates'. Tilly just talked and talked and we just sat and listened. At first, I had felt uncomfortable listening to her story. I felt out of depth as pregnancy was not a topic that I had confronted before. However, I felt that if I had been in Tilly's position that is what I would have liked someone to do... to listen and certainly not to judge.

She shared with us how her mother had died after a long battle with breast cancer. She explained how terrible it was for her to lose her mum, especially as she had no sisters, only her father and a younger brother at home. She had been very close to her mum and she was missing her dreadfully, even more so now that she was pregnant.

When she had first met Jacques, and she realised there was a spark between them, all she had wanted to do was to be with him. It had helped her fill the dreadfully empty space inside her. She told us, that being with him had made her feel important, wanted and loved. She said, "I felt complete, something I've not felt since mum died."

She continued to tell us that her father had found the death of her mum very hard to take and had kept his emotions to himself, not wanting to talk to Tilly about her mum or how he felt about losing his wife. He became totally self-absorbed, depressed and appeared disinterested in everything. That included Tilly and her brother. This made the death doubly hard to accept.

In the beginning, Jacques had been there for her, and then, she had found out she was pregnant. She had been horrified, had at first tried to ignore the tell tale symptoms and had hoped it was a false alarm. She told us that she had read that periods sometimes stopped when girls were under a lot of stress. However, as the weeks went by, her long awaited period failed to return, she began to feel sick every morning and knew with certainty she was in big trouble.

We both sat glued to our seats as Tilly continued. She told us that playing the flute had always been her passion. It was at the top of her list of important things she HAD to do. It wasn't a choice, something that she had any control over. I told her, I felt the same thing about my singing and I could tell by Immie's head nodding in agreement that she felt the same about her piano playing.

Tilly shared with us, "How stupid can you get? I had dreams of travelling the world performing at concerts in New York and London and then I'd take a break to perform on cruise ships as a solo artist." She sighed deeply, "Now, it looks as though it was all a pipe dream."

Jacques' mum, Cynthia, had suspected that Tilly was pregnant before Tilly had opened up to her. She had heard from Tilly that the relationship between Tilly and her father was almost nonexistent so, owing to the circumstances, she had taken matters into her own hands. She had offered Tilly a home. Tilly had gratefully accepted as it was the only option open to her. She admitted that although Jacques' parents were very kind to her, that the situation wasn't an easy one. For a start, it wasn't her home. She didn't feel as though she could be herself and worse, was the realisation that perhaps Jacques wasn't the person she felt she wanted to stay with.

The more she was getting to know Jacques, the further apart they were becoming. He couldn't understand why she was so upset at having to leave the Academy. He thought that as long as they were together, that was all that mattered. He found her being constantly sick, hard to take. She wasn't as much fun as she used to be and she didn't feel up to going out with him all of the time. She told us she believed she had been in love with him, but had now realised it was only a crush.

Is it a crush?
Or is it love?
A relationship in a rush,
Am I too young to know?
Shall I stay or shall I go?
Only time will tell.

"What a fool I am!" she exclaimed. "I can't admit to Jacques or his mother that I don't really want to have the baby. Cynthia is SO excited about becoming a grandmother. It's her sole topic of conversation and she keeps broadcasting the latest updates to all of her friends. I just wish she would give the topic a rest. I feel very muddled about it all and can't share her enthusiasm for the baby. My emotions are on a rollercoaster. I don't want to give the baby up for adoption. I couldn't do that, but it's such a responsibility and I don't feel ready for it. I've really messed up big time."

Both of us sat there in silence. We didn't know what to say. How can you say anything that is going to make the person feel better? The situation was completely out of our experience. We both gave Tilly a hug and told her we'd look out for her again and we could meet at the Coffee Shop for another chat.

On our return, I went in search of Gillie and relayed the story of Tilly to her. A thought had crossed my mind, perhaps it would be a good idea for Tilly to have some counselling. She was a brilliant flautist. It would be such a waste of her talent if she wasn't given the opportunity to continue to study the flute after she had the baby. Even so, it makes you think about her situation. I did not envy her at all. It made you feel that you'd want to avoid anything like it happening to yourself. Just one incident can have such a massive impact on the rest of your life.

I wasn't in the mood to settle to doing any work. I had borrowed an old guitar from the Block and with the few chords Simon had taught me, I took it out of its case and let my mind wander on a course of its own.

> Just seventeen,
> Full of hopes and dreams.
> I thought I had it all.
>
> Life's merry go round
> Has broken down.
> Where do I go from here?
>
> Washed away,
> A river of tears,
> Drowned in a flood of fears.

Poor Tilly. Love always, Amanda

Term 3 Entry 13

Dear H,

With all of this activity going on regarding the fund raising disco, you would think that I never do any work! Well, you are mistaken. As I mentioned before, we have to keep up our academic standards otherwise, we lose our place at the Academy. We also have exams looming ahead in Term 4.

Gillie has been running around organising the disco as well as doing all of her Housemother duties, plus teaching and writing her own songs. I just don't know how she fits it all in. She had previously cleared the date for the disco with the Head of the Academy and booked the hall and printed the posters, which Immie and I had spread around the village. Any available shop window was now proudly displaying the brightly coloured posters. She told me, at the last song writing session, that she'd contacted the local paper. The update is that they have now promised to send a reporter along with his camera and that he'll probably want to take a photo of Simon, Immie and me. She's also contacted the local radio station and asked if they'd feature the story plus airing the single of 'The Daisy Chain' on a segment they run for local news. She's plastered details on the News section of the Academy website and given updates on their Facebook page. So now, we have to leave it in the hands of these people and hope that the disco will be a sell-out!!

Meanwhile, we have to plod along as normal and pretend that nothing exciting is happening in the background.

Go with the flow!
Amanda

Term 3 Entry 14

Dear H,

The 'three of us', you know who I mean, have been in the limelight for the past two weeks. Having our photos in the newspaper and having the CD played on local radio has made us mini celebrities! It has not gone unnoticed by some people, especially Jessica who, at the present time, appears to have returned to being spiteful, noisier and even more disagreeable than ever. Gillie has advised us to ignore all negative comments, which we are trying to do, but it's not easy. Gillie reminded us, "Don't forget why we are organising this concert. It's to raise money for a good cause. Nothing should stand in its way."

Anyway, it's spoiling it for us, so I will be pleased when it's over. Have you ever tried to do something good and everyone thinks you are doing it purely to become famous? Well, that's ridiculous. It's not like that at all. I just wanted to help anyone who is being bullied. I don't want anyone else to go through what I went through. I only have to think about when I was being bullied by Cassandra and her more recent behaviour towards her step-sisters and I have shivers running up and down my spine.

Thankfully, the end of Term 3 is getting closer. We can then go home and everyone will have forgotten about it when we return. We hope.

Talking of Cassandra, it reminds me that Annabelle told Mum that Cassandra had eventually realised she wasn't going to win her battle to return home if she continued with her nightly displays of sobbing and hysterics. However, she hadn't given in without a fight. Annabelle was horrified when she last saw Cassandra and discovered that she had visited the local piercing salon that afternoon on her way home from school. Defiantly, she was now proudly displaying a ring through her nostrils. Aunt Rose had not yet returned from work. When she did arrive home she was greeted by a furious Annabelle who was in the process of texting Dominic. Cassandra had reacted to her mother's outburst of hysterics by threatening to 'go one worse' and have a 'Bite Back' tattoo where everyone would see it. There was lots of shouting, screaming, stamping of feet and tears from Cassandra until Dominic appeared in the midst of the uproar. He instructed Cassandra, in no uncertain terms, to calm down, grow up and go to her room until she could act sensibly. At first, Cassandra was reluctant to follow her father's orders. She stood defiantly with her feet firmly planted on the ground, arms folded and staring him straight in the face, she questioned him with, "Well, what are you going to do about it?"

Her father replied, "If you don't do as I ask, we'll send you away where you won't cause us anymore trouble. Go upstairs and when you've calmed down, we'll have a talk but not until you can control yourself."

Annabelle told Mum that Cassandra had taken her father's words to heart. She had unwillingly stomped up the stairs to her room where she had sobbed uncontrollably for a considerable time. To a background of, "I hate everyone!" and "No one understands me!" the adults had sat downstairs trying to block out the tirade blasting from Cassandra's room by drinking copious amounts of coffee and trying to make decisions on what was the best thing to do, both for Cassandra and for themselves. Everyone agreed that the situation could not continue.

Eventually, Cassandra had calmed down enough for her father to be able to lead her downstairs. She appeared, with very blotchy, puffy red eyes, but subdued enough to discuss her behaviour. It was agreed, for the present time, to leave Cassandra with Aunt Rose and change the therapist, on the understanding that if there were any more piercings, and definitely NO tattoos, that the situation would be reviewed on a monthly basis instead of the six months previously arranged.

Cassandra remains extremely unhappy living with her aunt but seems more settled and appears to have realised that she just has to stay and face the consequences of her actions. Hopefully, the new therapy will work. Cassandra appears to prefer discussing her problems with the new therapist and is now attending a group where she is being taught methods of dealing with her stress and anxieties.

Annabelle shared with Mum the fact that Dominic had been horrified that his beloved daughter would have a 'Bite Back' tattoo imprinted on her perfect skin. He had told Annabelle that he found the idea of his beautiful daughter disfiguring herself in that way sickening. Annabelle told Mum, "When crunch comes to crunch, it doesn't matter what Cassandra does, she will always be Dominic's princess even though she doesn't realise it."

Dominic had admitted, "I really don't know how to deal with this."

What a mess!
Amanda

Term 3 Entry 15

Dear H,

This term has swept by in a whirlwind of activity. It only seems a few days ago that Immie and I were boarding the plane back to the Academy. Now it's only another five days and we'll both be off to the airport again, but catching planes to different destinations.

The fund raising disco was a huge success. Gillie had certainly woven her magic to create an event resulting in an atmosphere that I would describe as 'electric glitz'. I don't think Mum, with her experience of 'themes' could have excelled on the final production. There seemed to be flashing electric lights of every colour and glitter balls hanging from the exposed beams in the hall ceiling. Gillie had even arranged, via a friend who owed her a favour, for a revolving circular dance floor with lighting to be temporarily installed. It was amazing! People had been encouraged to dress in their most sparkling outfits. It was truly magical, certainly, a night to remember.

Thanks to the media spotlight on the event, the hall was crammed to capacity with people who were so enthusiastic and supportive of raising funds for the Daisy Chain. We could have sold double the amount of tickets if the hall had been large enough to fit everyone in. The CD sold well. Gillie is talking about a much larger event for next year. Remember, she originally talked about two discos a year; she's now thinking of holding some sort of event once a year but bigger and better than this one and holding it in the city at an upmarket venue!! Phew!

I hope she's planning on organising the event herself!

The positive thing is that it has highlighted the Daisy Chain. Although there are already Daisy Chains operating, there are now more people who are aware of how important it is to have a support group for those being bullied. Since the night of the disco, there has been a lot of interest shown from students in the Academy. Charlotte gave us the impression that she was keen to learn more. She's been going through a really tough time.

Looking back to when I first began writing to you, I would never have believed that I could come this far. I have far more confidence than I had when I first began writing to you. Of course, I still have my doubts and my ups and downs. I'm not perfect. However, I now value friendship and support. Also to be so involved in something you love doing is certainly a good way to keep your mind active and stop any niggling thoughts from popping out.

Happy holidays. Amanda

Spring Holiday, Entry 1.

Dear H,

I've decided that I'm desperately in need of a rest. Life is SO FULL ON at the Academy. I sometimes wonder how we fit everything in. Mum said I looked peaky and thought I had lost weight. "We don't want you becoming ill," she said looking concerned.

"I'll be fine. I just need lots of sleep," I replied trying to stifle a yawn.

"Well, it's an early night for you then," she said kindly, "and there's no need to set the alarm. Stay in bed as late as you want. You don't have to get up early."

"No fear of that," I thought to myself.

A few days later

I didn't make much of an effort to do anything strenuous for the first few days. I spent lots of time lounging around catching up on movies I'd missed out on and listening to music. I still stayed up quite late but woke up later which I can only manage at weekends at St C's. I still managed my nine hours of sleep, which, I read, teens are supposed to sleep per night. It's certainly paid off as I've begun to feel less of a wreck and my pale cheeks now have more of a glow to them. (No need to wear blusher at the moment!) However, I have managed to saunter down to the coffee shop in the afternoons where I've met up with Emma. It's great that she's now mobile and enjoys scooting along the pavements at high speed in her Purple People Eater! Anyone who dares get in the way, watch out!

I also rode my bike to Holly Field's house and filled her in on the latest news. She's always so keen to hear what I've been doing, and although she has a busy schedule, she always makes time for me to call round when I'm home. Apart from a much needed trip to Philippe's to have my hair trimmed and styled and a shopping trip with Mum, I've really enjoyed some down time.

Lazing around!

Amanda

Term 4 Entry 1

Dear H,

Well back to news of the Academy. As I mentioned earlier, this is the final term for the year. Who would believe it? Time has just flown by. It just shows you that you have to try to enjoy and experience every moment as much as you can.

This is going to be a MAMMOTH term! We have exams in five weeks and if we don't pass, we will be in big trouble. My scholarship states that I have to maintain a high standard in my academic work as well as in my Music studies otherwise, I will not be able to continue at the Academy. It puts an awful lot of pressure on me.

Then, there is the final concert for the year, even bigger and more splendid than the midyear concert. I also want to help Gillie to officially start the Daisy Chain and help with any fundraising with any other charities I can. Before I left for St C's, Mum gave a few words of advice, "Amanda, I know you want to help other people and I think that's great, but I think concentrating on the Daisy Chain is enough for you to be concerned with at the moment. You're doing a great job with that."

She's right as usual. Getting the Daisy Chain off the ground and running well is something I really want to do. I don't want to spoil things by not doing it properly.

Anyway, I can tell you now, there's not going to be much socialising until after the exams are finished. Immie and I have decided we'll limit ourselves to the events organised by the Academy for Saturday evenings. This week is a 'Welcome Back Disco' so we can't miss that especially if RELIEF is performing. Simon would never forgive us if we failed to turn up and give our support.

It's definitely an early night tonight!

What an exciting life we lead! LOL!

Amanda

Term 4 Entry 2

Dear H,

Every time we return to the Academy after a break, there's always a surprise awaiting us. Some are good and others aren't. This time, it concerns Jessica who is having a break from this term.

We've been told it's confidential but that she needs a rest. She hasn't left the Academy and there is a possibility that she may be returning next year. I think I mentioned earlier that she had been warned that if her grades weren't up to scratch, she would have to leave. We're not sure of what is happening. She was certainly showing signs of unusual behaviour last term, up one minute and down the next. There are all sorts of rumours flying about. Some of them are SO ridiculous, they are laughable, not that it's a laughing matter. It wasn't difficult to realise that she had a few problems. Hopefully, they can be sorted out. However, no one appears to be disappointed about her not being here. I would admit that life will be less stressful for Immie.

As there is only one term left of this academic year, we have been told that no one will be replacing Jessica.

Must unpack!
Amanda

Term 4 Entry 3

Dear H,

How am I going to fit everything in? I've made a list of priorities. I rang Gran last night in a bit of a panic. To say it was a 'bit' of a panic was an understatement. She advised me to work out a study plan spending more time on the subjects I feel are the weakest.

Gillie has taken control of the Daisy Chain for the moment so that's something I don't have to concern myself with until after the exams. To begin, we plan to have one meeting a week, unless there's a special need to have more. We've decided to meet every Wednesday evening. The first meeting will be in Gillie's flat, away from prying eyes. I'll let you know how it goes.

Looking forward to it but am not quite sure what to expect.

In anticipation,

Amanda

Term 4 Entry 4

Dear H,

Well, we've held our first official meeting of the Daisy Chain! I'm so relieved to say that it went off very well. We didn't expect a lot of people as it wasn't planned to be an open meeting where anyone can just turn up. That's not how the Daisy Chain works.

However, prior to the meeting, a few students who had never given me any idea that they were, or had been bullied, indicated they wanted to speak privately with me. Some had pushed notes under my door. I was SO amazed. Students who had given me the impression that they had everything under control, as well as those who gave off an air of confidence, asked me if they could be present at the first meeting. Most students confided that they had kept the bullying a secret even from their closest friends and relatives. I suppose, this is the effect that bullies have on their victims. A lot of bullies threaten their victims, so those being bullied aren't going to make a big fuss about it. They just end up suffering in silence. When I was a student at St Ursula's, I believed I was the only one suffering from bullying, but from what people are telling me, it's a universal thing and certainly not to be under estimated.

The positive thing about the Daisy Chain is that there is support for those being bullied and that people can speak in confidence and without fear.

I thought I ought to call into Gillie's flat to alert her about the numbers who may be attending the meeting. She told me, "Don't worry Amanda, nothing surprises me. We'll cope with two or twenty."

In the end, ten students arrived. Some people who had indicated they were going to attend failed to turn up. Gillie said that was quite normal and that we may see more attending further down the track.

The meeting was really to establish what role the Daisy Chain was going to play in the lives of its members. Gillie talked through the list of objectives which I'd originally made with Emma. We were all given a printout and discussed each point. Everyone agreed that what they needed was support and to be able to talk with someone who had been in similar circumstances and who understood. They also wanted knowledge of the best way to react to the bullies. We felt that the feeling of isolation resulting from the bullying was almost as bad as the bullying itself.

The meeting closed at 9pm. Gillie asked anyone to stay behind if they were experiencing any particular problems so that they could write their names on a list so she could contact them at a later date. A few people mentioned that they were no longer being bullied but that their problems and insecurities had not been dealt with adequately and that they still had issues.

Everyone appeared to be interested in the Daisy Chain pendant and Gillie told us she would inquire about purchasing some. Other people felt that they weren't interested in the pendant as it would identify them as having been bullied. I could see their point.

Generally speaking, I think the first meeting went well but only time will tell.

Feeling positive.
Amanda

Term 4 Entry 5

Dear H,

The program for the big end of year super-duper concert was planned last term by the Music Department, so we already know which pieces we are going to perform. After the exams have finished, I understand that our academic work for the year ends and we put all of our efforts into rehearsals for the concert.

Just have to concentrate and pass the exams first!!

Amanda

Term 4 Entry 6

Dear H,

Brilliant! Our recording of 'The Daisy Chain' on the local radio was such a success that we've been asked to record it backed by the whole orchestra. This isn't as simple as it sounds as the backing music has to be arranged for each instrument and that takes time. The plans are for the recording to take place around the end of term. The orchestra will be rehearsing for the BIG concert so it shouldn't be a problem to slot in another piece of music. As I mentioned before, the program for the concert has been arranged for a while, so the orchestra is already familiar with the music for the concert. Then the Director of Music at the Academy got rather carried away and suggested that it would be a good idea if the whole of the concert was recorded.

There are rumours of a professional video/recording company being hired for the occasion. We'll wait and see!!!

Changing the topic, Immie and I have decided to give Zumba a go for our Sports Option this term. It's only once a week and we thought a music based activity would be enjoyable. As we have heard Zumba can be strenuous, we thought it would be a way to work off our nervous energy. I'm still trying to fit in my cycling BUT, I must admit, I don't seem to have the time to fit it in very often at present.

We're now going for a walk to the village. Immie and I feel as though we need a break before dinner. Then it's back to the revision timetable... French this evening.

If anyone had suggested this time last year that I would be living such a busy life, I wouldn't have believed them. Neither would I have believed that I'd have been able to cope with everything. I suppose you never know what you CAN do unless you try. I must admit, sometimes I wish we weren't quite so busy and life wasn't so frantic.

From Busy Bee,

Amanda

Term 4 Entry 7

Dear H,

Every time Immie and I walk to the village, we look out for
Tilly but we haven't seen her for a while, not in fact since we
had the long conversation in the coffee shop. I often think
about her and hope she's OK. It won't be that long before
the baby is born. I'm sure it's due before Christmas. I would
absolutely hate to be in her position. Living with people who
are not family and who you don't really know well, must be
very hard. Some of the students have said Jacques has been
seen out with another girl but I don't know whether it's
true or not or whether they are just delighting in spreading
unkind gossip. It seems that the relationship between Tilly and
Jacques was perhaps over before it began.

Short and sweet!

Amanda

Term 4 Entry 8

Dear H,

Such exciting news! Remember I mentioned about 'The Daisy Chain' being recorded at the final concert for the year? Well, it's even better than that.

A notice has been pinned to the main notice board in the Block that we are to be aware that a famous producer will be attending the concert. The notice states that he's on a talent scouting mission. A brand new musical is being planned to premiere next year in the city. The producer is coming to watch the concert with the idea that he may ask suitable students to audition for some of the roles. One is for the major role but they require a male for that, so that counts me out! There are also parts for minor roles and for these both males and females are required. This news has certainly created a fair amount of excitement as well as jealousy! Here we go again with the 'I'm better than you,' syndrome.

When I mentioned this to Mum she was rather hesitant. She said she had read in the newspaper that auditions had already been held in some of the cities. The article stated that if you are successful enough to be selected for a role, the producer then arranges for all of those people to gather in one central city for three months of intensive rehearsals before the show premieres. Mum said, '"Just wait and see what happens Amanda. You've got an awful lot on at the moment."

I don't think she's keen but it would be great to be selected. I'm not suggesting that I would be good enough. There are lots of other very talented students here - but still it's exciting all the same.

Anyway, I've got exams to get through first so I'd better concentrate on my revision as we have another meeting of the Daisy Chain tomorrow evening.

Imagination running riot!

Amanda

Term 4 Entry 9

Dear H,

Gillie has invited some special guests to come to talk to us at
our Daisy Chain meeting this evening. At our last meeting she
mentioned that she was keen to arrange mentors for some
students although who these students are has been kept
confidential. She's just amazing. She doesn't have to do all
of this. Her workload is heavy as it is. We are just so lucky to
have her at St C's.

I know Charlotte is experiencing problems with some of
the guys who live in the village. They tend to hang around
in groups chain smoking on the main street especially near
the coffee shop. I've heard them mimicking her speech. Just
recently, she hasn't wanted to go to the coffee shop with
us and has been making excuses not to walk into the village.
I didn't take much notice at first. However, things suddenly
clicked with me when a small group of us had a break from
study and wandered down to the coffee shop. The guys were
as usual lounging around on the opposite side of the road.

In a really rough voice one called out, "Where's Ch...Ch...
Charlotte? Is she too scared to walk down the street? Have
we frightened her?" This was followed by raucous laughter and
then the whole group chanting, "Ch...Ch...Charlotte, Ch...Ch...
Charlotte! Cat caught your tongue?"

I was horrified. I felt icy cold shivers running down my spine. I was reminded instantly of Cassandra and her gang and how they had tormented me by shouting, 'Piggy, fat bum,' from the bus window. My thoughts returned to that moment when all I had wanted to do was to crawl up into a tiny ball and roll away and never be seen again. How cruel can people be? It's not surprising that Charlotte hasn't wanted to walk into the village with us. I'm not sure what to do. I'll have to have a talk to Gillie about it.

Time for dinner and then off to the meeting.

Living in hope,

Amanda

Term 4 Entry 10

Dear H,

Quite a few invited guests turned up to the meeting of the Daisy Chain. As our group is only for girls, Gillie had restricted her invitations initially to female guests only. I had imagined, for some reason, and was dreading, that they would be old and frumpy, but I need not have been concerned. Some were young and trendy, and the older ones weren't frumpy at all. What a relief! I should never have doubted Gillie's ability in her selection of suitable mentors.

What amazes me is how many people Gillie appears to know. I don't know how she does it! She asked the guests to introduce themselves to us in turn. The three younger ones turned out to be Uni students from the various Universities in the city. They were all studying Psychology and one, we were told, was in the final year of her PhD studies. Of the five older ladies, three of the guests had professional backgrounds, and the remaining two, were people who just wanted to help. The interesting thing about all of them was that they stated that they could remember bullying incidents in their past. Some admitted to being bullied themselves when they were young and others shared stories of their friends and relatives who had been bullied.

Didi, one of the older ladies, stated that her granddaughter had been bullied relentlessly at school. It had resulted in severe problems in later life and that was her reason for offering to help members of the group in any way she could. One lady, Jan, admitted to having been bullied at her place of work. I think we were all surprised by that. I know I was. I had associated bullying only where children were concerned. The common thread amongst the group was that each person had felt so alone, didn't know how to cope with the bullying and that few people had told anyone else about it whilst it was happening. The most horrifying aspect of all this, was that the bullies always appeared to win and NOTHING appeared to happen to them.

I noticed that at the end of the meeting, Gillie called Charlotte over and quietly introduced her to Didi.

What an interesting and positive evening!

Amanda

Term 4 Entry 11

Dear H,

Gillie stopped to speak to me in the corridor as I was going down for dinner last evening. She asked me how I thought the meeting had gone. I told her I'd really enjoyed it and found it useful. I'd asked some of the other girls who had attended what they thought. They all agreed that we were on the right track.

Gillie then went on to ask whether either Immie or I had seen any more of Tilly. I replied that we'd looked out for her in the village every time we'd walked there but we hadn't seen anything of her, not even coming to the Academy for her flute lesson.

However, it seemed strange that after my conversation the previous evening with Gillie, who we should see in the village this afternoon but Tilly. When Immie and I sauntered down to the village, we caught sight of her hurrying away from the Post Office. She gave the impression she didn't want anyone to recognise her. She was wearing a sunhat with a wide brim and a dull coloured billowing sundress. We called out her name and rushed to catch up with her. She hesitantly stopped and turned around to see who had called out to her. We were both shocked by her appearance. I only hope it didn't show on our faces. She looked more like a woman in her mid to late twenties than in her teens. Although she had a prominent bump, she appeared to have lost weight and looked very fragile. She was very pale and the fine lines on her forehead and around her eyes clearly showed her anxiety. The 'old' Tilly that we had known at the Academy had disappeared. It was SO sad.

We invited her to join us for a coffee but she shook her head. "I don't want anyone to see me like this," she whispered pointing to her enlarged stomach and with that she turned and walked quickly away.

That evening, I couldn't stop thinking about her. I knocked on Gillie's door and told her the news. She expressed her sorrow but said, "I can't interfere even though I would like to help. Tilly is no longer a student here so there is little I can do."

Feeling helpless,

Amanda

Term 4 Entry 12

Dear H,

Gran phoned the other evening. She asked me how things were going. After I'd talked nonstop for ten minutes about how full-on everything was, she said, "It sounds to me as though it would do you good to have a weekend away before the exams begin."

I replied immediately, "Oh, that would be wonderful but I can't spare the time."

"Amanda, knowing you as I do, you are completely up to date with your revision and a break would do you good. I'm not just inviting you, I'm inviting Immie and I'm certain what her reply will be."

"Oh Gran, you are an angel as well as being my Fairy Godmother. I'll go to speak to Immie."

I raced to find Immie and told her the good news. She replied, "I'm pleased you have decided to come. Your Gran contacted me first as she said you'd find an excuse not to go."

I was SO surprised, "She didn't!"

"Yes, she did. See what we have to do to stop you working!

Anyway, my mum has already given permission so all we need to do is contact your Mum and ask Gillie's permission."

With that, we both rushed around gaining permission and making arrangements with Gran. It was all done so quickly and Gillie thought it was a good idea for us both to get away and have a weekend of fun.

So excited!

Amanda

Term 4 Entry 13

Dear H,

Sadly, now we're back! Time always seems to fly by when you're having fun. The weekend was really great. I feel so much better for having had a break from the Academy.

Gran didn't put any pressure on us to do anything. She seems to be a mind reader. She realised we were both completely exhausted and wanted to lounge around and not have anything special organised. However, when she mentioned, "I'd thought of going into the city to have a look around the sales but I don't suppose you two would be interested?"

We looked at her in astonishment and then noticed the unmistakable twinkle in her eyes. Isn't it amazing how you can suddenly find the energy to walk for miles around shops!! Well, perhaps that's an exaggeration, but we seemed to walk a long way and surprisingly, we also appeared to gain the energy to carry various bags of new clothes back to Gran's car!

Apart from the shopping trip, we did catch up on some much needed sleep.

Ready to take on the world!
Amanda

Term 4 Entry 14

Dear H,

Mum rang last evening to wish me 'Good Luck' in the exams which begin today. She said, "Dad sends his Best Wishes too."

That really cheered me up. Mum always describes my Dad as 'a man of few words'. He feels things very deeply but doesn't show it very often. Mum continued, "When you've finished the exams, we've an idea we want to discuss with you. I think you'll like it. There's nothing to worry about."

After the phone call, I kept wondering what she was referring to. I wish people wouldn't do that... leave you in suspense racking your brains and trying to work out what it is they are going to discuss with me. I haven't a clue.

Emma sent a text, "Break a leg! Love Emma xx"

I thought that was a saying for an actor before they go on stage, not for someone due to take a French exam!!! Gran also phoned last evening. "All the best darling. Don't worry about a thing. I know you'll do well."

I wish I had her confidence. Anyway, talk to you next week when it's all over.

I'd better finish now. My French exam is due to begin in 45 minutes time, so I'd better stop wondering and walk over to the examination room.

Wish me luck!
Amanda

Term 4 Entry 15

Dear H,

Here I am again! Thankfully, all exams are over and we're now anxiously waiting for the results. Such a relief not having exams looming over you! The atmosphere around the place has changed dramatically. Everyone is smiling again. It may seem strange to you, but we now have five weeks devoted solely to our music and the end of year concert. It's all go in a big way.

We've also received some really exciting news! "Not again?" I can hear you asking!

The Academy is in the process of arranging an overseas trip for the end of next year. The program has yet to be finalised but the general idea is that a select group will be taken to tour and put on concerts in the UK. THEN, the group is to visit one or two places in Europe yet to be arranged. The idea is that those lucky enough to be invited to go on the trip will fly first to London. They will travel to various venues in the UK where they'll perform, but the rest of the time will be dedicated to sightseeing. Then, the lucky ones will travel on the Eurostar, which is a very fast train that travels from London to Paris in less than two and a half hours. This part of the trip has yet to be finalised. However, I did notice a visit to La Scala in Milan, Italy was on the agenda!! I would imagine that was the idea contributed by Signora De Luca, the Italian teacher who has made up her mind I'm going to be an opera singer. I THINK NOT!!

I won't bore you with all of the details here but I must admit, I would LOVE to go. So much is hanging on this end of year concert!! We've got the recording of the whole concert with 'The Daisy Chain' song included! Then, we have the producer attending who is coming to watch to see if he thinks any of us are good enough to audition for his musical. THEN, on top of all of this, we now have the Music Specialist teachers eyeing us up and down like hawks to make selections for the overseas trip! Originally, I was mad keen on being selected for the musical, BUT NOW, I desperately want to be selected to perform in the UK.

Mum says she thinks it's all a bit too much of a good thing. She thinks the Academy puts enough pressure on us anyway without all of this extra stuff. She told me, "Amanda, you are, after all, only 14. I'd like you to have more free time to enjoy yourself. Sometimes, I'd like to pull you off the fast track."

I understand what she's trying to say. The college does put us 'under the pump'. If I didn't enjoy what I'm doing so much, I would have begged my parents to let me leave by now, BUT I do love the singing and all that goes with it. I love the whole 'set-up' and wouldn't want it any other way. When I think back, I can't believe that I've coped so well this year, especially when I consider what I was like at St Ursula's. I'm not the same person, well I must be, but the real me that was hidden away, deep inside me has bubbled up to the surface. It's really amazing.

From a 'bubbling',

Amanda!!!

Term 4 Entry 16

Dear H,

Even though the whole time table has altered, we are still
continuing with our Daisy Chain meetings. Last night, we had
a visiting speaker who talked about Bullying and Depression.
I wish I'd been a member of the Daisy Chain when I was
experiencing bullying. It would have helped so much.

People requiring mentors have now been allocated to suitable
people. We are all encouraged to show our support to other
members by talking to them and being around if they appear
vulnerable. Some of our members are no longer being bullied
but have the scars from previous episodes. After the bullying
is over, it can reappear later in so many forms. I've read
of people who have long term depression and suffer from
anxiety. I'm sure there are lots of other side effects. One
person has been referred on to specialist help. It is a relief to
know that anyone who requires help will not be left to cope
on their own and that some of the money raised from our
concert has gone towards specialist treatment.

Gillie has suggested that money raised by the sales from the
CD recording of the concert will be donated to this fund.

Mum says she's going to phone me later this evening to tell
me what it is that she and Dad are so excited about. Still no

idea what she's talking about.

Surprises always fill me with dread! Well, not long to wait now.

Amanda

Term 4 Entry 17

Dear H,

Thankfully, the news wasn't anything to be frightened about.
Mum began the conversation by saying that she and Dad
had felt uncomfortable with the fact I was a scholarship
girl when they had the money to pay for my tuition at the
Academy. SO, they have decided to offer a Scholarship for the
next five years for any student, male or female who shows
exceptional promise in the area of Vocal Studies. I was thrilled
as I have felt awkward at times with the fact that all my
fees are being paid for me. However, I would never have come
to the Academy if Holly Field, my original singing teacher, had
not encouraged me to enter the singing competition where I
was awarded the Scholarship. Mum said the Scholarship would
be officially announced at the end of the concert, but that it
was a secret and I was not to tell anyone, not even Immie.

I felt ecstatic with the news. I've long realised that achieving
a place here is a great privilege. There must be lots of
students throughout the country who would do anything for
a place. If Mum and Dad can assist another student, it would
be terrific.

Lips sealed!
Amanda

Term 4 Entry 18

Dear H,

SUCH exciting news!! How could I forget to describe the disco held to celebrate the end of exams! This was held as usual in the pergola area of Sherwood House. However, this time, it had an unexpected twist!

Everything was going along fine. People were tucking into the vast amounts of food and drink and when they weren't eating, they were on the dance floor. Everyone was well into the celebrations when above the music, which was LOUD, were heard sirens warbling and wailing through the night air. The next thing we knew was that we were surrounded by police cars with red and blue lights flashing which brightened up the whole area. In actual fact, there were only two cars, but at the time, it seemed very dramatic and gave us the impression of lots more cars. Four policemen, fully armed, stepped out of the vehicles and proceeded purposely towards the pergola. However, by now, the music had abruptly stopped and before we knew what was happening, one of the senior boys had set off at a rapid pace into the darkness with all of the police in close pursuit.

At first, the reaction was stunned silence. The piercing sirens had by now been turned off and the music was on hold. This was followed, seconds later, by a few girls becoming hysterical and sending their high pitched screams through the night air. Then the evening became even more dramatic when the girlfriend of the student, who was being chased, fainted on the spot. It was all over in five minutes but it seemed to go on for ages. The student didn't stand a chance of escaping with four able-bodied policemen chasing him in hot pursuit, especially, as by then, some of the security guards, hired by the college had joined in.

I think it was the highlight of the year, as nothing like this had ever happened before. The student was soon apprehended. By then, the Head of the Academy, Dr Hathaway, and some senior teachers had been alerted by all the noise and had arrived on the scene. The police explained to them that the student had been in involved with a gang from the village in supplying and distributing drugs. The Police had plenty of hard evidence and a thorough search of his room confirmed their suspicions.

We were all dumbstruck. Everyone entering the Academy had been warned time and time again, that drugs were banned and that anyone having any involvement with drugs would have some explaining to the police and of course, be expelled from the Academy.

After a short lecture from one of the senior staff, the evening's events were cut short and we were told to return to our respective boarding houses. The rooms of the boys were then searched by members of staff before they were allowed back into their residence.

Of course, everyone was far too excited to go to sleep that night. Conversations in the kitchen on our corridor continued until the early hours. Slices of hot buttered toast spread with strawberry jam followed by chocolate biscuits were drowned by mugs of hot chocolate and coffee. Everyone had their own interpretation of what had happened and how they thought something had been 'going on'. However, no one could officially give any concrete evidence. From my point of view, I must have been the only one who didn't know anything or, hadn't heard anything etc.

Eventually, Gillie appeared and told us she couldn't get to sleep with all of the noise we were making. It was by now, very late, and we were told to go to bed immediately.

We later learned that the group involved with the drugs was exactly the same gang who had been tormenting Charlotte and had caused her so much anguish. I don't think she need worry about them again as they are all awaiting court appearances.

The girlfriend who fainted was also questioned, and her room searched, but there appeared to be no evidence of her knowing anything about her boyfriend's dealings with drugs. I think she seemed as surprised and shocked about it as we all were. We later heard that she's been allowed to continue with her studies at the Academy under strict conditions that she had no further contact with her boyfriend.

I heard her say, "Well, he wasn't really my boyfriend. I was going to dump him anyway."

I don't think anyone believed her!

Charlotte told me she is relieved that she can now go to the coffee shop with us without the fear of being jeered at. Didi is working with her to help with relaxation techniques and also giving her tips on how to deal with her stammer.

I must phone Emma tomorrow!!! She will think I've forgotten her. Not long now until the end of term and I can spend lots of time with her.

SO MUCH TO TELL!

Amanda

Term 4 Entry 19

Dear H,

Rehearsals are now in full swing. However, the pace has
slowed down considerably. This is due to the fact that
we have no lessons and the pieces that we are playing at
the concert were previously selected so we know them
well. However, the aim is for us to now perfect them.
Everything has to be spot on as we are being videoed and
the webcam will be live. Simon, Immie and I also have to
rehearse 'The Daisy Chain' for the recording of the CD
with the whole orchestra. This will be done at a separate
time.

Of course, everyone is aware that the famous director
will be attending the concert. SOME people seem to think
they've already been chosen before the event as they are
SO talented. I think SOME people may be very disappointed.

The Academy will be making their selections on the
overseas group after they have viewed our exam results,
spoken to our specialist music tutors and watched us
perform at the concert. The students offered places will
be informed before everyone leaves for the long summer
holiday. I'm not holding my breath although I think Immie
stands a chance.

We'll just have to wait and see. I'm beginning to sound just like my Mum!

Fingers crossed.

Amanda.

Term 4 Entry 20

Dear H,

Well, the school year is nearly over. We have rehearsals daily for the BIG EVENT! Everyone is hyped up with excitement and the atmosphere is alive and buzzing with electricity, if you know what I mean. Tensions are running high amongst the final year students who are all waiting impatiently to hear if their applications to various musical conservatories have been accepted. Some students have decided to have a gap year and go travelling before committing themselves to more study.

The final event of the year is the Christmas Ball. This is held on the last night before we break up for the Christmas holidays. Simon asked me to go with him as his partner. Of course I accepted immediately without thinking and later realised what I'd done. The invitation had come out of the blue... so unexpectedly. I had just assumed I would turn up with Immie. I was really surprised, flattered and nervous all at the same time. I hurried along to Immie's room to share the news.

"Why are you so surprised?" she asked.

"Wel... Simon's just a friend," I stammered.

"What's the problem then?" she queried innocently.

I felt my face blush with embarrassment, "Well, it makes things different doesn't it?"

"I don't understand you sometimes. If he's a friend, then just go with him as a friend."

"Well, what about you? You'll have to go on your own."

"No, I won't. I've got a partner!" she exclaimed with a smirk from ear to ear.

"WHO?" I asked in astonishment.

"You'll just have to wait and see," she replied before flouncing out of her room and leaving me standing rooted to the spot.

Life is full of surprises!

Amanda

Term 4 Entry 21

Dear H,

I was rather nervous telling Mum that I'd been invited to the Christmas Ball. Her immediate reaction was, "What are you going to wear?"

Strange, I was sure she was going to inquire who had invited me and give me a list of advice, but no. I replied that I hadn't thought about what I was going to wear. It had been the last thing on my mind owing to my confusion over the invitation. She suggested I give her some ideas and then she'd have some sketches done. I could then choose and she'd have the design made up for me. She told me that although it was short notice, she could still manage to have the dress made up and bring it with her when she and Dad visit for the concert. I replied that she didn't need to go to so much trouble but she assured me it was no bother. I'll have a word with Immie and ask her what she's thinking of wearing.

I'd be quite content with going into the city and finding something for myself, but typical Mum always has to have her input into anything connected with fashion.

Mum also mentioned an update on the dreaded Cassandra. Mum didn't want me to be concerned that Cassandra might be allowed home for Christmas and that I may see her around. Well, it appears that according to her mother, Annabelle, there has been an improvement in her behaviour. Dominic has been visiting Cassandra at Aunt Rose's and spending time with her. Her parents have agreed that she may have a break from staying with Rose. Annabelle has decided to take Cassandra away for Christmas, so thankfully, she won't be around. That's one less thing to worry about.

From a relieved Amanda

Term 4 Entry 22

Dear H,

Well, everything is going well. We've been continuing to hold unofficial weekly meetings of the Daisy Chain. The itinerary for the first term for next year has been planned although we need to finalise some of the guest speakers. Gillie said she'd do that during the holiday.

Our rehearsals have been building up in intensity and we have the final rehearsal for the concert tomorrow with the concert the following evening. Mum and Dad are flying over and Gran has made arrangements to drive. They have booked into the same hotel as last time. Immie and Simon's parents have also booked in so it will be almost like a family reunion.

Immie and I decided it would be more fun if we went into the city and chose our own dresses for the ball. The college had arranged for a bus to take a group into the city last Saturday afternoon so we tagged along. I don't think Mum was too pleased when I told her. When I explained that Immie needed a new dress as well, and that I would feel uncomfortable wearing one specially designed for me, she saw my point. We had a terrific time trailing around the shops until we found exactly what we were searching for. Immie did her usual trick and had to try on just about every dress she saw. I was shattered by the time we arrived back at St C's.

Anyway, Immie will be wearing a burnt gold shiny number and I'll be in a dark jade embroidered top and matching jade skirt... long of course!

Can't wait!

Amanda

Term 4 Entry 23

Dear H,

What a blast! I've been living in a whirlwind and am still floating up in the clouds. The concert was just fantastic. After a nerve racking dress-rehearsal, where everything that could go wrong, did go wrong, the final concert went off perfectly. What a relief ... especially as the webinar could be viewed live from anywhere in the world! We have been told, the famous producer was most impressed, although we are still unsure exactly who he is. However, he will be contacting the Academy to discuss possible applicants for his musical.

At the end of the concert, Dr Hathaway stood up to give his annual speech. Thankfully, it didn't go on for too long. He has a reputation for 'liking the sound of his own voice' a bit too much. Anyway, he was in a very good mood. After praising all of us, he continued to praise some of the final year students who have attained coveted places at some of the best conservatoriums in the world.

He then closed by announcing the special scholarship being offered by Mum and Dad. Of course, this was not a surprise to me, but what followed was. Gran had also decided to offer a scholarship to any student who was exceptionally gifted in piano. It was quite an emotional moment for me and as the applause died down, I realised I had tears of joy running down my cheeks.

The next morning, we all met up for coffee and the most scrumptious cakes at the hotel before the parents all made their way home. Mum appeared to be having an animated conversation with Immie and Simon's parents so we'll wait to see what, if anything, she is planning this time. I wish she wasn't such an organiser!

Flying high!

Amanda

Term 4 Entry 24

Dear H,

Everyone is becoming so emotional. Now that all the tension of the concert is over, it has just hit the final year students that they are leaving and that they will be saying goodbye to all of their friends. As the Academy takes students from all over the world, it may be difficult for some of them to keep in close contact. The girls are all going around sobbing and hugging each other.

It suddenly made me realise that this time next year Simon will be leaving. I've grown so used to him being around, not all the time of course as he has his own friends, but he's always there to give me support if I need it. The older you get the more complicated life becomes. I sound really old, don't I? I really will miss him, but let's not go there. There is another year before that happens AND tonight is the CHRISTMAS BALL!!!

SO EXCITED!

Amanda

Term 4 Entry 25

Dear H,

I just couldn't believe it.. Immie's ball partner!! Guess who?
Remember at the beginning of the year she sat next to
Patrick at the theatre? Well, it would appear she's changed
her mind about him and when he asked her if she would go to
the ball with him, she changed from a demure sophisticated
young lady into a typical giggling teenager. All the times when
he's tried to chat her up throughout the year and she's tried
everything to avoid him and now this!!

Anyway, we had a wonderful time at the ball. First of all there
was a buffet followed by dancing. The event began formally
and ended up just like a posh disco. The Academy had hired a
professional band so that everyone could have a night off.
It was great fun, a special night to remember before we
all parted to go our separate ways and join our families for
Christmas.

Other news to share is that Immie, Simon and I have been
offered places on the trip to Europe! I can't believe it.

What a year it has been. When I was at St Ursula's, I never
imagined that my life could change so much. It's not been
easy, leaving home and having to cope with the pressure that
the Academy puts us through, but I've coped. I've not done

it on my own. There's you, Dear H, my confidant at all times, I can't thank you enough. Then there's Emma and Immie, Simon, the supplier of tissues, the wonderful, understanding Gillie who guides us all through our rough patches and lastly, there's my family who have travelled this journey with me every step of the way. A HUGE thank you to you all!

There's so much to look forward to!

See you next year.

Love always,

Amanda xx

THE DAISY CHAIN

Little daisy
Standing alone
In a field with a greenish hue,
Battered by the wind and rain.
Is that you?
Is that you?

Little daisy
Standing forlorn
Ready waiting to be reborn,
Left to nature's beck and call.
Trampled, torn,
Trampled, torn.

Little daisy,
How many seeds
Scattered throughout on hill and plain
Nurtured by the gentle rain?
Daisy Chain,
Daisy Chain.

PTO

<u>Chorus</u>

Step by step, side by side

Come join the Daisy Chain.

Join us and we'll be your guide

Help you hold your head up high.

Together, we'll step out, speak out,

Fight the foe

And put the bullies to shame!

To Dennis,
For his deep understanding of the trials of a writer!

Thank you to Steve, Brenda, Imogen, Leila and Holly
for your valued contributions.

ISBN: 978-0-6480822-1-7

© Diane Guntrip 2017

www.dianeguntrip.com

Layout and design by All In One Book Design (www.allinonebookdesign.com.au)